"You're right. I am pregnant."

"And it's mine."

It wasn't a question and Miranda didn't insult Warren by trying to lie to him again. "Yes." She would have liked to look at him, to see how he took it, but couldn't bring herself to do so.

Warren put his hand on her arm, turning her to face him, but his touch was gentle now. "We'd better start getting to know each other very quickly."

Miranda dragged her eyes up to meet his, her own scared and vulnerable. He was regarding her steadily, and she felt that there was even a trace of self-mockery in the way his mouth twisted. "Why?" she asked warily.

"So that we're not quite such strangers when we get married!"

SALLY WENTWORTH began her publishing career at a Fleet Street newspaper in London, where she thrived in the hectic atmosphere. After her marriage, she and her husband moved to rural Hertfordshire, where Sally had been raised. Although she worked for the publisher of a group of magazines, the day soon came when her own writing claimed her energy and time.

Books by Sally Wentworth

SALLY WENTWORTH

The Devil's Kiss

Harlequin Books

TORONTO • NEW YORK • LONDON
AMSTERDAM • PARIS • SYDNEY • HAMBURG
STOCKHOLM • ATHENS • TOKYO • MILAN
MADRID • WARSAW • BUDAPEST • AUCKLAND

Harlequin Presents first edition December 1992
ISBN 0-373-11517-2

Original hardcover edition published in 1991
by Mills & Boon Limited

THE DEVIL'S KISS

CHAPTER ONE

IT WAS nearly three-thirty before Miranda's business lunch finally broke up. She glanced at her watch with a small frown, having been hoping to have finished before this. But the meeting had been successful, and it didn't pay to hurry; when you were headhunting a man in the hope of persuading him to change jobs you had to let him take his time and patiently answer all his questions, relevant or otherwise. And in this case relocation was involved, so that the man had a whole list of queries that his wife had sent along, too.

As soon as she'd said goodbye to her guest, Miranda hurried across to the telephone booths in the foyer of the restaurant and called up her own answering machine at the flat. That abrupt call from Rosalind just as she had been on the point of leaving the office this morning still troubled her. But it was probably nothing important. Her sister, after not bothering to get in touch for weeks, would often make panic calls, usually because she needed to borrow something, money or clothes mostly. And she always made it sound as if it would be the end of the world unless she got what she wanted immediately. But there had been something in Rosalind's voice this morning that had seemed to go deeper than the usual panic, a note of urgency when she'd said, 'I can't talk to you at work. I'll phone you at the flat. Please be there as soon as you can. I *have* to talk to you, Miranda.'

The number connected and the answerphone switched itself on. Miranda pressed the button on her remote control handset and the answerphone began to play back the messages. There were two business calls from people she was headhunting, agreeing to meet her for further discussions, and she made a note to ring them back. Then Rosalind's voice came on the line. 'I'm in London. I wasn't going to tell you; I was going to manage it alone. But then I—I needed someone to go with me.' A sob broke from her. 'Oh, Miranda, I'm pregnant. I—I've come down to London to have an abortion. I can't keep it, you see. The—the baby. He—he wouldn't stand by me.' Fresh sounds of weeping came as Miranda listened in horrified dismay to her sister's disjointed voice over the line. 'I'm going to the clinic now. Please come if you can. Oh, Miranda, I'm scared.'

She gave the address of the clinic, the words so broken by crying that Miranda could hardly hear. That was the trouble with an answerphone; you couldn't ask it to speak more clearly. But she noted the address down as best she could, and, frantic with worry, ran out of the restaurant, pushing in front of the startled doorman to grab a taxi he'd just found for a customer. 'Sorry, but it's an emergency.'

The cabby gave her an annoyed frown; evidently she didn't look as affluent as his lost fare. 'All right, where to?' he demanded as he pulled out into the Strand. Miranda gave him the name of the clinic. 'Never heard of it,' he said with unhelpful satisfaction.

'I think it's in Portman or Portland Road.'

'Well, make up your mind; there's a couple of dozen roads by that name in London.'

Miranda glared at the back of his head. 'Well, if you don't know then radio in and ask. And quickly, please; I'm in a hurry.'

But it was a good half-hour before the taxi eventually pulled up outside the clinic. Miranda paid off the driver and ran inside. A girl looked up from her desk as she pushed the door open and hurried in, her high heels echoing on the marble floor of the reception area. 'Good afternoon. Are you late for an appointment?'

'No. I believe my sister is here. Rosalind Leigh.'

'Oh, yes. She came in this morning.'

'Where is she? Has she—has she had the operation yet?'

'I imagine so. Just a minute, I'll check.' The girl picked up the internal phone while Miranda waited in an agony of impatience. 'Yes, she has.' The girl smiled at her as if she ought to be pleased. 'She's fine. She's back in her room now.'

'I want to see her.'

'Well, she's probably still a bit woozy, so——'

'I want to see her *now*,' Miranda said on a fierce note of command.

The girl gave her a surprised look, not used to that much self-assertion from a contemporary. 'All right. She's in room 206 on the second floor. The lift's over in the corner to your right.'

Miranda didn't bother to wait for the lift but ran up the stairs as fast as her figure-hugging skirt would allow her, and walked straight into room 206, too worried to knock.

Rosalind was lying on her side in the bed, like the foetus she'd just deliberately had taken away.

Pushing that thought aside, Miranda went up to her. 'Hi. Are you awake?'

'Miranda?'

'Mm. How are you feeling?'

'OK, I suppose.' The younger girl gave a great unhappy sigh, then said wretchedly, 'I had to do it. There was just no other way.' And added belligerently, 'I hate being a woman. I just hate it, hate it, hate it!'

Taking hold of her hand, Miranda gently stroked the hair from her sister's pale face. 'You'll feel differently when this is all over,' she said comfortingly. There were a load of questions she wanted to ask but this wasn't the time. Rosalind began to cry in deep, heartbroken distress, so Miranda took her in her arms, holding her, murmuring words of encouragement, but her heart seethed with anger at the man who'd done this to her young sister.

Eventually Rosalind fell asleep. Miranda laid her back on the pillow and looked round the room. It was small and contained only the basic bed, small wardrobe and bedside cabinet, but there was a tiny bathroom opening off it and everything was new and clean. On the whole, for this sort of place, it was quite luxurious, and Miranda guessed that it must be a private clinic. Which made her wonder how much it had cost Rosalind to come here and where she'd got the money.

She stayed by her sister's bedside, sitting quietly in outward patience, but inwardly Miranda was full of anger and distress. Anger that this should have happened at all and distress that Rosalind hadn't confided in her earlier. Although there was a six-year age-gap and they hadn't seen very much of each other since Rosalind had been at university,

Miranda had still thought they were quite close, and it grieved her to think that Rosalind had even contemplated going through such a traumatic experience without telling her, let alone asking her help and advice.

After half an hour or so a nurse came in to take Rosalind's pulse and blood-pressure, waking her up. When she'd gone the younger girl lay back against the pillows, looking pale and drawn.

'Would you like a drink?' Miranda asked anxiously.

'Please.' Rosalind nodded.

She heaved herself into a sitting position but her hands were unsteady and Miranda had to help her to hold the glass. Afterwards Miranda took her hand and said, 'Want to tell me about it?'

'What is there to tell?' Rosalind answered on a bitter note. 'It's the age-old story: boy meets girl, gets girl pregnant, then clears out—fast!'

'Were you in love with him?'

Dark shadows filled Rosalind's eyes at the question. 'I thought I was. And if the next question is "Did I think he was in love with me?", then, yes, I really thought he was.'

Taking her hand, Miranda looked earnestly into her sister's face. 'Why didn't you tell me?'

A flush came into her pale cheeks and Rosalind lowered her head, picking at the bed-cover with her free hand. 'You're always so in control of your life,' she said in a slow, wretched tone. 'You'd never let a thing like this happen to you. I—I tried to think of it as no big deal. I told myself I could cope alone. That I'd got myself into this mess so I must get myself out of it, but—but...' Her voice broke and Rosalind burst into tears again.

Putting her arms round her, Miranda said, 'You crazy little chump. What are big sisters for if not to go to when you're in trouble? You must have known I'd help you in whatever you decided to do.'

'I—I suppose so, but you're always so busy. You're never at home when I call.'

For a brief moment Miranda felt a stab of guilt, but almost immediately suppressed it. It was true that she had a full and busy lifestyle, but she always felt that she had her priorities right, and family always came first, so she said firmly, 'But you know that I always have time for you. If I'd known there was anything wrong I would have dropped everything and gone up to York immediately. You do know that, don't you, Roz, darling?'

After a moment, Rosalind nodded, then sighed, and said, 'I wanted to be as strong as you over this. But I'm not, I'm so weak compared to you.'

'No, you're not,' her sister said firmly. 'You're just a lot younger, that's all. And who could be unemotional about something like this, for heaven's sake?' They were silent for a few moments, each thinking their own unhappy thoughts, until Miranda said, 'I take it you haven't told the parents?' And when Rosalind shook her head, 'Well, I can't say I blame you; they'd only worry themselves sick about whether you were doing the right thing.'

As she spoke Miranda looked at the younger girl closely, wondering whether Rosalind had any reservations herself, and saw a sad look come into her eyes.

'You—you didn't consider keeping the baby?' she asked hesitantly.

'Yes, of course I did,' Rosalind answered shortly. 'But—but he was completely against it. He said it was a stupid idea to saddle myself with a baby when I was still at university. He said it would ruin my whole life.'

On a practical level Miranda had to agree with that, but it would take a very hard-hearted woman to see the position so clear-mindedly at such an emotional time. And it would certainly take someone far more worldly than her young and gentle sister.

'He didn't offer to marry you, or take on the responsibility of the baby, then?'

'No. He made that quite clear,' Rosalind answered in bitter, raw pain. 'He said that if I decided to keep it he would have nothing to do with it, ever.'

Miranda felt another flash of hatred for the man who had treated Rosalind with such cold ruthlessness, and said, 'This man—your boyfriend, is he another student?'

Rosalind was silent for a moment, then shook her head. 'No. I—I met him here, in London, when I was staying with you in the summer vacation.'

Her eyes widening in surprise, Miranda said in a shocked voice, 'You're not saying he's one of my friends?'

'No, of course not.' Rosalind was quick to deny it. 'I met him by chance.'

'Who is he?'

Rosalind hesitated, then shook her head. 'It doesn't matter who he is. I just want to forget him. I just—just want to forget that this whole thing ever happened.'

Tears came into her eyes again and Miranda squeezed her hand comfortingly. 'Of course you do, darling. Don't worry about it. Everything's going to be fine. As soon as they let you out of here we'll go back to my place and you can stay until you feel well enough to go back to college.'

But although she spoke so soothingly, Miranda felt venomous towards the unknown man. He must be quite a bit older than her sister, she surmised—and quite used to dealing with a situation like this, from the sound of it. Miranda would have liked to ask more questions but Rosalind had closed her eyes and she knew this was the wrong time. She would have to wait until she'd taken Rosalind home to the flat and she'd had a chance to recover before she could ask anything more. And even then Rosalind might not tell her the man's name; her sister had an obstinate streak in her at times. Which was probably one of the reasons why she hadn't come to Miranda for help sooner. Glancing at her watch, Miranda wondered how long it would be before the clinic would want them to leave.

This thought sent her in search of one of the staff. She found a woman in nurse's uniform in an office down the corridor, sitting at a desk and busily writing up a report. The woman looked at her with world-weary eyes as Miranda walked in. 'Yes?'

'I'm Rosalind Leigh's sister. When will she be well enough to leave?'

The nurse consulted an open diary on her desk. 'Let's see; she had the operation at midday so she could leave later tonight, but she's booked in to stay overnight.'

'Really?' Miranda frowned, thinking that Rosalind only had her student grant and the money she earned from a part-time job, which would hardly be enough for a place like this. Unless the man had paid. Hoping to find out his name, she said casually, 'Who booked her in?'

'I'm afraid we're not allowed to give that information,' the nurse said primly.

Miranda gave her a calculating look; the woman might well only be working in a place like this because she needed the money. Taking a twenty-pound note from her bag, she said, 'Perhaps you have a favourite charity you would care to give this to?' And she laid the note on the desk.

'Yes, I suppose I could find one, thank you.' The woman took a file from a cabinet behind her and took out a printed form, putting it down on the desk. 'If you'll excuse me for a moment; I've just remembered I have to check on a patient.' She went out, picking up the money on the way and slipping it into her pocket.

The form was obviously a standard one and contained Rosalind's name, age et cetera. Her address was just given as York University. But it was the method of payment that drew Miranda's eyes. The account was to be charged to someone named Warren Hunter, who had elected to pay by credit card, but there was no address. So at least Rosalind's boyfriend had had the decency to pay for the abortion. The knowledge should have given her some satisfaction, but strangely it only made her more angry. Dropping the form back on the desk, Miranda turned away, but paused in the doorway. Warren Hunter: she was sure she'd heard that name somewhere before. She sifted through her mental files, again afraid that Rosalind might have met the man through her, but, although she usually had an extremely good memory, she couldn't come up with anything.

Going back into Rosalind's room, she found her awake and said gently, 'You're booked in to stay overnight. Did you know that?' And when Rosalind nodded, 'I'm sure that's best. Look, you're tired, so I'm going to leave you now to get some sleep. I'll go home and get a bedroom all ready for you, then I'll come back and visit you again this evening. And tomorrow I'll come and collect you as soon as they say you can go. Is that OK? If you'd rather I stayed with you, then I will. You only have to say.'

'No.' Rosalind sighed, then managed a smile. 'I'll be OK.' Wistfully, she said, 'I wish I were more like you.'

'Well, that's a crazy thing to wish for. You're you; I'm me. And I happen to like my kid sister the way she is, so just stay that way, will you?' She bent to kiss the younger girl's forehead. 'Now, you go to sleep and I'll see you later.'

'OK. Bye.'

Miranda went to the door and opened it, but paused to look back. Rosalind's head was already drooping, her face almost as pale as the pillow and deep shadows of unhappiness around her eyes. It would take ages for her to get over this, Miranda thought angrily, if she ever did get over it. It wasn't the kind of thing a woman with any sensitivity could ever forget, or forgive herself for—not if you were by nature as warm-hearted and gentle as Rosalind. This hateful man had robbed her not only of her innocence but also of her self-respect and the trust she'd had in others. If Miranda had been able to at that moment, she would cheerfully have wrung this Warren Hunter's neck!

Miranda did go back to her flat, but first she called in at the office and phoned her two contacts, arranging to meet them for lunch on successive days during the following week. Hopefully, by that time Rosalind would be well enough to be left for a few hours. She then rang one of the researchers who worked on a freelance basis for the company. 'Hello, there. I wonder if you'd take on a private job for me? I'm trying to track down a man named Warren Hunter. No, I don't know who he works for or even where he lives, but I think it's here in London. I think he's youngish, probably under thirty-five. And I'm sure I've heard the name before, but I can't think in what connection.' She laughed. 'Yes, I know it will be like looking for the proverbial needle, but if anyone can do it you can. OK, thanks a lot. Would you phone me at home if you find him?' She hesitated, then added, 'And I'd rather you didn't mention anything about this to Graham.'

Graham Allen was her boss, a partner in the firm, and also her steady boyfriend for almost a year. But this was Rosalind's secret and Miranda had no intention of betraying her confidence, even to someone as close as Graham.

After dealing with the most imperative work on her desk, Miranda swept the rest into her briefcase to take home to work on. One of the big advantages of her job was that a great deal of it could be handled at home over the telephone. Switching off the lights in her office, she looked in on the secretary she shared with two colleagues. 'Give Graham a message for me when he comes in, will you, Megan? Tell him I'm sorry, but something's come up and I won't be able to meet him tonight.'

'Do you want me to tell him what it is?'

'No, just that I can't make it.'

Hurrying out of the office, Miranda glanced at her watch. Just time to catch the florist before it shut. There she bought two huge bouquets of flowers for Rosalind, and handmade chocolates from a nearby shop, hoping that they would cheer the girl up. Carrying her purchases, she walked to the edge of the kerb to look for a taxi. It was dusk already, the autumn nights lengthening, but the street was well lit and she stood out against the crowd, tall and slim in her tailored business suit, her long fair hair falling in a glistening bell to her shoulders. A cab appeared out of nowhere and drove her the few miles to her flat in a newly converted warehouse in Docklands.

The flat was big, spacious, with a great deal of character, and Miranda was very proud of it. It had cost the earth, of course, but she was earning really good money now and felt that she could afford it. Working quickly, she made up the bed in the spare room, using her prettiest sheets, afterwards splitting one of the bouquets between several vases so that the room looked full of flowers. Her meal that evening was a freezer-to-microwave one; she was too anxious to get back to Rosalind to spare the time to cook, and by seven she was on her way back to the clinic, the second bouquet in her arms.

This visit was better because Rosalind wasn't so tired and Miranda even managed to make her laugh a few times. But she was still low enough to be pathetically grateful to her for coming and for the presents.

'You spoil me,' Rosalind said huskily as she bent to smell the flowers.

'Nonsense, who else do I have to spoil?'

Miranda stayed until she was turned out by one of the nurses at nine o'clock, and was confident that Rosalind was feeling far less miserable. The subject of her boyfriend had been carefully avoided by them both; Rosalind because she was ashamed and embarrassed, and Miranda because she didn't want to upset her sister again. When Miranda got back to her flat there were two messages from Graham on her answerphone: one just saying that he'd called, and the other to tell her that he was going out to dinner at their favourite restaurant and would be there until ten if she could join him. Glancing at the big old factory clock that she'd picked up cheaply in a flea market and now dominated her entrance wall, Miranda saw that it was only nine-thirty. She hesitated for only a moment, then called a cab.

They had been to the restaurant, a small place near London Bridge, just by the river, so many times that the proprietor greeted her by name. He beamed when he saw her. 'Miranda! We were afraid you weren't going to make it. Graham's at your usual table. Can I get the waiter to bring you anything?'

'Just coffee, thanks.'

Graham stood up as soon as he saw her, then put his hand on her arm to draw her to him and kiss her lightly, but possessively, on the lips. 'Hello, darling.' His eyes ran over her, noticing that she was still wearing the suit that she'd worn to the office that morning. 'What was the emergency— someone change their mind at the last minute?'

Sitting down in the chair that the proprietor had pulled out for her, Miranda waited until he'd gone before she shook her head. 'It was nothing to do with work. A family crisis.'

'Oh?' Graham raised his eyebrows. 'Nothing wrong with your parents, I hope?'

'No, they're fine.'

He waited, but she didn't go on and his mouth twisted slightly. The waiter brought her coffee and Miranda changed the subject by telling Graham about her two new contacts. 'They seem to be exactly what the design company are looking for.'

Graham had also reached the coffee stage and was sipping the one cup that he allowed himself in an evening; he prided himself on keeping fit and laid down rules that he lived by, which was the reason they came to this restaurant so often; it specialised in fish, which a dietician friend of Graham's had told him was vital for good health. He also went jogging every morning and worked out in a gym twice a week. It was just as well he did, because headhunters had to spend a lot of time talking to employers and their potential employees, and the best time to talk was usually over a meal or a drink, when everything was more relaxed.

Headhunters also had to be astute readers of mood and Graham recognised a 'KEEP OUT' sign when he heard one, so he fell in with the change of topic and discussed work until they were ready to leave. 'Care to come back to my place for an hour or so?' he suggested.

'Thanks, but I'd rather go straight home.' They emerged on to the pavement and Miranda shivered, feeling the first nip of winter in the air. They walked quickly over to Graham's car, a new Jaguar. He always drove Jaguars and traded them in for a new model every year. As they drove along Miranda said, 'I think I'll work from home for the next few days, if that's OK with you.'

He gave her a sharp glance. 'Is this because of the family crisis? If you want some time off——'

'No. That's been—dealt with.'

She didn't explain further and Graham said rather stiffly, 'I realise that it's none of my business, but if I can help in any way——'

Recognising that he was put out, Miranda quickly turned to smile at him and touch his arm. 'That's very sweet of you, Graham, and I do appreciate your concern, you know that. No, I just want to be available at home for a few days, that's all.'

He was obviously disappointed that she wasn't going to confide in him, but Miranda had an idea that this was because he didn't like her having secrets from him rather than because he seriously thought that he could help. Although if she'd asked him to help she knew that he would have done so willingly enough.

When they reached the converted wharf he insisted on going up in the lift with her to her flat. Graham preferred to live further out in the suburbs, and had a small, but extremely expensive, modern flat in Wimbledon, within walking distance of the All England Lawn Tennis Club where the famous championships were held every year. He disapproved of her living in Docklands, saying that it wasn't a settled community and there was too much friction between the original dockers' families, who had lived there in long terraces of small houses for generations, and the incomers, the thousands of career-orientated young people who were tired of commuting into London and massed on to the Docklands development like bees in a new swarm.

Maybe he was right; Miranda only knew that she loved living there and would never have been able to afford a place with such a large living area anywhere else. So far she hadn't experienced any trouble at all, but Graham still insisted on seeing her safely back to her flat whenever they went out together. Most times she appreciated the gesture, though it nearly always meant that she had to invite Graham in for a nightcap, but tonight she didn't want that and his insistence irritated her a little.

She glanced at him as they stood in the lift. She wasn't very tall herself, only five feet four—plus another two or three inches for her high heels—but Graham wasn't a lot taller. His figure was on the hefty side and he had constantly to watch his weight, hence the food fads, whereas Miranda had a very slim, almost boyish figure, and never put on an ounce no matter what she ate. Sometimes she thought that he had first become interested in her because she was short enough for him to look down on. There had been occasions before they had started going out together when she'd seen him eyeing up tall, willowy model girls with a wistful look on his face.

When they reached her door Miranda turned to him and said firmly, 'Thanks for bringing me home, Graham, but I'm not going to ask you in this evening, if you don't mind. It's been a rather traumatic day and I'm tired.'

'All right, I understand, but at least let me come inside for a moment so that we can say goodnight.'

He kissed her with his usual blend of efficiency and possessiveness, only reluctantly letting her go when she drew away. When he'd gone, Miranda thankfully ran a bath and lay in it, gazing up at the ceiling, free to worry about Rosalind again. Hopefully, once her sister got back to university and involved in college life again, she would get over this unhappiness. But it would take a long time before she got her confidence back; her confidence and trust in men, anyway. And Miranda could hardly blame her. Whoever the man was who'd done this to her, he must be a complete swine. He must have realised how innocent Rosalind was and yet he hadn't even had the decency to make sure that she didn't get pregnant. Her thoughts became angry again, and Miranda resolved to find this Warren Hunter—find him and make darn sure that he paid in some way for what he'd done.

But Miranda had to control her impatience until almost three days later before her researcher had any news for her. Rosalind was still staying with her at the flat so, saying that it was business, Miranda took the call on the extension in the bedroom. 'What have you found out?' she asked eagerly.

'Well, your Warren Hunter is quite a high-flier. I found his name in our own files. We tried to headhunt him once ourselves, some years ago, which is where you probably heard the name, if you read up the old files when you joined the company. He's a computer consultant and a couple of firms were very keen to get him, but he turned our overtures down flat and has since started up his own business. I've managed to talk to a few people and they say he's doing extremely well; that the business has a great future.'

'What's the name of the company?' Miranda asked sharply, an idea beginning to form.

'Compass Consultants; it's in Compass Road, you see.'

'Mm. Clever. Who's he got working for him?'

'An extremely good team, evidently.'

'And what about Hunter himself?' Miranda asked, lowering her voice even though Rosalind had the television on. 'What did you find out? Is he— is he married?'

It wasn't an unusual question for the researcher to be asked; whether a potential employee was married and had children or not often made a big difference to their willingness to change jobs. 'No, and with no serious ties that I can find out.'

'A playboy?'

'Could be, but he's more interested in building up his company as far as I've heard. Do you want me to send you the details?'

'Please. I want as much information as you can possibly get about his company, even down to the secretaries and the tea-lady. And if you could bring it along here, I'd be very grateful.'

'OK. When?'

'How about now?'

He laughed. 'You career girls are all the same; get your teeth into something and you can't wait to get to work on it.'

But he brought the file of information round the next day and Miranda again took it into her bedroom to study in detail. She spent most time going through the list of employees of the company, then made a few phone calls to the office, the idea she'd had taking a more definite shape. But before she put it into operation Miranda wanted to make absolutely sure that this Warren Hunter and Rosalind's boyfriend were one and the same.

She had tried to persuade Rosalind to go out with her to see a film or for a meal several times, but the younger girl refused, still too miserable to want to go out. So the next evening they were sitting together at home as usual watching a video film, but when it was over Miranda firmly leaned forward and switched off the television. 'Roz, I think it's time we talked about your future.'

'You mean it's time I went back to York,' Rosalind said with a little grimace.

'You said it, I didn't.'

'No—I can't sit moping around here for the rest of my life, can I?' the younger girl sighed.

'Quite right,' Miranda said briskly. 'And if you don't go back to college soon you'll have loads of catching up to do. And when you get there you must cram every minute with as many activities as you can find so that you don't have time to think of this. Maybe even some work, too.' She grinned. 'And before you know where you are it will just seem like a bad dream.'

'Do you really think so?' Rosalind asked, desperate for reassurance.

'I'm certain of it.' Realising that it was now or never, Miranda began, 'The man, your boyfriend.' She held up a hand when Rosalind opened her mouth in protest. 'It's all right, I'm not going to ask you his name. I just wanted to know whether there's any chance of your seeing him again.'

'No,' Rosalind returned with fierce emphasis.

'But you might run into him accidentally in York.'

Her sister shook her head, pushing her long fair hair off her face. 'No, I only ever went out with him while I was here in London in the summer.'

'How long did you go out with him?'

'Nearly the whole six weeks I was here.'

'Why didn't I meet him, then?'

'If you remember, you were away on business most of the time, and—he was away part of the time as well, so you just didn't coincide.'

'I see.' Angry at the necessity but anxious to make sure that she had the right man, Miranda pursued, 'What kind of man is he?'

Rosalind's face shadowed. 'Older than me. Very sophisticated, and very good-looking. I'd never met anyone like him before. I—I know it sounds corny to say it, but he completely swept me off my feet. I was just so amazed that he was interested in me. I thought that he was far more likely to go for someone like you than me. He was so ambitious and successful.'

'Successful?' Miranda asked, hiding her dismay at what the last two sentences had revealed of Rosalind's ideas about herself.

'Yes, he's the director of a company.'

'What kind of company?'

'Something to do with computers.' She looked at Miranda. 'I know that's true because I rang him there a couple of times.'

Miranda would have dearly loved to have asked the name of the company but was afraid to push Rosalind too far; however, she was already sure that she had the right Warren Hunter. 'Did he say that he was in love with you?'

'Yes, he did, but only when—when...' Her voice broke and she couldn't go on.

When they were making love, Miranda guessed. 'It's OK, I understand. When did he break it off?'

'He didn't, not really. When I went back to college he promised to write and to come up and see me, but he didn't. And when I tried to phone him I only ever got his answerphone, and he never answered my letters.'

'Did you manage to tell him about the baby?' Miranda asked, although she already knew the answer.

Rosalind nodded. 'I wrote to tell him, but when he didn't reply I rang him at his office and made a fuss until he came to the phone. That's when...' She turned away, biting her lip, and it was a few moments before she went on wretchedly, 'That's when he told me to have the abortion. He said he would book me into the clinic and to call him back. He had it all arranged within half an hour.'

Leaning forward in her chair, Miranda took Rosalind's hand and said, 'Well, maybe it was the right thing to do in the long run. Would you really have wanted the child of a man like that? Now you can go back to college and put the whole affair behind you. Just forget it.'

Rosalind gave her an agonised look. 'I'll never be able to forget. And I'm never going to trust a man again as long as I live.'

'Sure you will,' Miranda said with a smile. 'One day someone else will come along who you'll really fall in love with, and you'll know that he's the right man for you.'

'Like you with Graham?' her sister asked.

The question brought Miranda up short. 'It's a little early to say,' she prevaricated, and quickly changed the subject by saying, 'Why not stay here until the weekend, then I'll hire a car and drive you back to York?'

'You don't have to go to all that trouble; I can catch a train.'

'Nonsense, I'll enjoy the drive.'

Confident that her researcher had come up with the right man, Miranda had to wait until she'd taken Rosalind back to college before she could put her plan into operation. Using the information she'd acquired, Miranda carefully studied the details on the employees at Compass Consultants, working out who were the key men and women in the company. Next, she shamelessly used her own company's contacts to find employers in competition with Compass Consultants who were searching for people with similar qualifications. That done, Miranda psyched herself up to pick up the phone and call the first name on her list of employees, knowing that she had to get the contact interested within the first thirty seconds or lose him.

Cold-calling was always hard but Miranda was good at her job and the man agreed to meet her to discuss the offer further. She also made him promise not to mention it to anyone in his company; a routine precaution but especially important in this case. Great. Picking up the phone again, Miranda called the second person on her list.

Over the next few weeks Miranda headhunted seven people who were vital to Warren Hunter's company, gradually working up the hierarchy towards the top. And all of them she had persuaded to switch jobs and hand in their resignations on the same day, the first of December. Not that they knew about each other, of course. There was just one person left whom she wanted to lure away, a man called Jonathan Carter who was evidently Warren Hunter's right-hand man. He had been harder to entice, and it had taken several persistent calls before he had quite suddenly changed his mind and become interested enough to agree to meet her.

What she was doing was perfectly legal but it was far from ethical. Ordinarily she would never even have considered taking more than one employee from a firm, and Graham would have had a fit if he'd known what she was up to, but Graham's policy was not to interfere, and he trusted her completely. At times Miranda felt rather guilty, but she only had to remember Rosalind crying her heart out in the clinic for her to be as determined as ever that Warren Hunter deserved everything he was going to get.

Her meeting with Jonathan Carter was to take place in a discreet restaurant in Soho. Miranda had offered him the Savoy Grill, which was where she usually met the high-fliers, but he had stipulated this place instead. In her job Miranda had to be prepared to meet a contact anywhere, any time—had even met one man at the top of the Eiffel Tower—so she happily agreed. Wearing a long, swinging coat over a mohair sweater, culottes and boots, a stetson-style hat on her head, Miranda walked eagerly down the street leading to the restaurant, keyed up for the interview, knowing that if she could lure this man away with the others then Compass Consultants and Warren Hunter would be so badly hit that he might well go under, or at least have a terrible struggle to start again from the beginning.

The restaurant was dimly lit, and Miranda thought it more a place for assignations between married lovers than for a business meeting. Still, if that was what the man wanted, she wasn't going to argue. The head waiter took her coat and she perched on a stool at the small bar to wait; she found that contacts were usually late in the hope of convincing her that they weren't anxiously interested. But Jonathan Carter surprised her by being dead on time; he followed her into the restaurant after only a few minutes.

Miranda had given her guest's name to the head waiter and she turned as he brought the man over. Carter's appearance, too, was another surprise—and an agreeable one. Over six feet tall, broad-shouldered and muscular, he looked more like an outdoor man than a person stuck to a computer all day.

'Miss Leigh?'

Still sitting on her stool, Miranda held out her hand. 'How do you do?' He seemed to hesitate for a fraction of a second before shaking it, but then his grip was so firm that it made her wince. Miranda found herself looking up into dark grey eyes set in a sharply handsome face of strong jaw, high cheekbones and level brows. Right now his eyes were going over her in surprised assessment, but she was used to that; most people expected a female headhunter to be some sort of elderly ghoul and were always taken aback to be met by a young and pretty blonde.

'What will you have to drink?' she asked.

'Gin and tonic, please.'

She made her usual light conversation aimed at putting the person at ease while they drank, but he didn't say very much, and Miranda got the distinct impression that he was sizing her up. Which was fair enough; but she had learnt to be very sensitive to the undercurrents and she had the uncomfortable feeling that there was antagonism behind his rather withdrawn exterior.

When they'd finished their drinks they were shown to a corner table where they couldn't be overheard. Picking up the menu, Miranda said, 'They seem to have a good selection here. What would you like?'

'Just steak and a salad,' Jonathan Carter said without even looking at the menu.

'No starter?'

'No.'

Miranda gave him a surprised glance but gave her order for just a main course to the waiter.

'Let's get down to business, shall we?' Carter said as soon as he'd gone. 'I'd like you to go through the details of the offer once more.'

'All right.' Hiding her annoyance at his brusqueness, she carefully described the package she had to offer him. He listened in attentive silence, but showed no emotion, neither displeasure nor gratification. His attitude puzzled Miranda; he had been pretty hostile to the idea at first on the phone, but had seemed quite enthusiastic the last time she'd spoken to him. She knew that he was married and wondered if his wife had been nagging him one way or the other, that sometimes happened when relocation was involved, but the firm she hoped to place him with was again in London so that didn't apply in this case.

Their meal came before she'd finished but her guest seemed to have little appetite because he hardly touched his food, and frowned in impatience when she paused to eat.

When she'd finished outlining the proposal he asked one or two questions and then sat back in his chair, his eyes fixed intently on her face. 'Tell me, do you enjoy your job?'

It wasn't the first time she'd been asked the question. 'Yes, very much, as a matter of fact,' Miranda answered pleasantly, but again uneasily noting the coldness in his voice.

'Were you headhunted into it?'

She smiled. 'Everyone asks that.'

'I'm sorry to be so predictable.'

The antagonism was open in his voice now and Miranda tried not to show her concern as she smiled and said, 'Of course you're not; it's only natural to wonder. No, I drifted into it. Most people do.'

'And just what qualifications do you need to be a cannibal—sorry, headhunter?'

'We prefer to call ourselves executive search consultants.'

His mouth drew into a thin-lipped smile, the first she had seen him give, but there was no humour, only mockery in it. 'I'm sure you would,' he said sneeringly.

Realising that this was one she wasn't going to win and angry at his attitude, Miranda gave up trying and said, 'You haven't yet said whether you want to accept the offer.'

'You haven't yet told me what qualifications you need,' he retorted. 'Other than being young, blonde and nubile, that is,' he added insultingly.

Miranda's chin came up. 'I have a master's degree in business administration and had three years of hard experience in venture capital and industry generally before I came into the firm.'

Jonathan Carter suddenly sat forward, his face dark and menacing. 'And because of that you think you have the right to lure away a man who's vital to my company! Doesn't it ever occur to you to think about the effects of what you're doing? Of the hole you could be digging for the man's employer? But no, I don't suppose it does—all you're interested in is the commission,' he finished in strong disgust.

'But I don't understand.' Miranda gave him a bewildered look. 'You don't have any stake in Compass Consultants. Why should you care when you can get a better deal somewhere else?'

'Exactly! That sums up your whole attitude, doesn't it? But this time you made a big mistake. You came up against friendship and loyalty instead of greed.' Getting to his feet he glared down at her in cold fury. 'Because I'm not Jonathan Carter.'

She stared at him open-mouthed. 'But then who——?' She broke off, already knowing the answer.

'That's right. I'm Warren Hunter and I *own* Compass Consultants.'

CHAPTER TWO

MIRANDA stared at the man who stood towering
over her, a look of cold triumph in his grey eyes.
For a moment she was completely disconcerted by
the trick that had been played on her, but then the
realisation that she was face to face with the man
who had treated her sister so cruelly brought her
to her feet on a surge of fury. He was so tall that
he still towered over her but Miranda didn't let that
stop her. Leaning forward belligerently, she said,
'So *you're* Warren Hunter. I might have known.
You certainly look cold-blooded enough to treat
women the way you do.'

His left eyebrow rose mockingly. 'Trust a woman
to be a bad loser and take it personally.'

Anger tore through her; he was speaking of her,
of course, but his attitude could apply just as easily
to poor Rosalind. 'You louse!' she said clearly, not
caring who overheard. 'You think you're so damn
clever, don't you? You think you can just use
women and then throw them aside. You're
disgusting!'

Totally disconcerted by her attack, Warren drew
back, staring at her. 'What the hell——?'

But Miranda swept on, her fury rising. 'But this
is one time when you're not going to just walk away
from the destruction you've caused. This time
you're going to pay for what you've done. And I
don't mean just money. You're going to *really* pay.'

She paused for breath, angry colour in her cheeks, but Warren, as irate as her now, cut in, 'My God, I've heard that you career girls could get vicious, but, lady, you beat the rest hands down. Just because the deal you set up has fallen through and you've lost your commission——'

Miranda laughed in his face and glared at him across the table. Other diners were watching quite openly now and the head waiter was walking hurriedly towards them. Determined to embarrass Warren as much as she possibly could, Miranda said loudly, 'I don't give a damn about the commission. Just as you don't give a damn about the people you hurt, whose lives you wreck.'

'Aren't you being over-dramatic?' he sneered.

'No, I'm not. You ought to take the trouble to find out the surname of the women you use before you discard them.'

His eyes widened in surprise but then drew into a sharp frown. 'And just what is that supposed to mean?' There was menace in Warren's voice now but he hadn't bothered to lower it, apparently indifferent to the watchers.

The head waiter had come up and tried to interrupt them. 'Please sir, madam, if you could——'

But he was swept aside with an imperative wave of Warren's hand. 'Well?'

'It means,' Miranda said furiously, her hazel eyes flashing fire, 'that this is one time when you're not going to get away with discarding a girl you've seduced like some—some toy you've used and grown tired of.'

'What the hell are you talking about?'

'As if you didn't know!'

'No, I don't, so tell me.' He leaned forward, putting his hands on the table, bringing his angry face nearer to her own level.

But Miranda had become aware of the people watching them with avid curiosity and realised that she didn't want the world to know Rosalind's secret. And just in time she remembered that she mustn't give away the other deals she had made with his employees in case Hunter thwarted those, too. So instead of answering, she swung her bag on her shoulder and strode past him towards the door.

His hand shot out and grabbed her arm, but Miranda swung round and said, 'Take your hand off me,' so fiercely, that for a moment Warren was so taken aback that his grip loosened and she was able to wrench her arm free and walk on.

The waiter, getting his priorities right, came rushing after her, getting in Warren's way as he also tried to catch her up. 'Madam, the bill?'

Miranda stopped, and turned, bringing them up short. 'He's paying,' she said forcefully, her arm outstretched as she pointed at Warren. 'By credit card—the same way that he pays for his girlfriends to have abortions!'

The whole restaurant fell into a stunned silence, broken only by the bang of the door as Miranda slammed it on her way out. Still on a tide of anger, she strode to the kerb and only had to wait a few moments before a taxi came along. As it drew away she saw Warren rush out of the restaurant and run across the pavement after her. But it was too late; the taxi sped away and had soon pulled into the busy main road to Piccadilly Circus and the web of streets that led from it.

Miranda sat back in her seat with some satisfaction, feeling that she had definitely emerged the winner from that conflict. Although it was a bitter disappointment that Jonathan Carter had proved to be more loyal to Warren Hunter than to his own interests. Now her plan to bring Compass Consultants to the edge of ruin wouldn't be so effective, but she comforted herself that it would still be a great blow. Instead of turning the tables on her, as he'd thought, Warren Hunter would find that he had a major crisis of his own to deal with. Maybe that would take his mind off young girls for a while, Miranda thought triumphantly.

Her mind went back over the incident. She ought to have realised who he was sooner; the antagonism had been so apparent. She was one woman he definitely hadn't set out to charm. But she could see now how easy it had been for Rosalind to fall under his spell. To a young girl, used only to her fellow students, Hunter must have seemed from a different planet; self-confident, successful, and very good-looking in that hard, lean way that women always went for. Even someone like herself, a career-girl with some experience of the world, could hardly be blamed if she fell for him, Miranda realised. Which was enough to make your flesh creep when she thought of what type of man he was.

Having an unexpected hour to herself, Miranda went to Knightsbridge and spent the time shopping for Christmas presents before going back to the office. She felt good; having that confrontation with Warren Hunter had been a whole lot more satisfying than getting back at him from a distance. She felt no regrets about it whatsoever. And worse, from his point of view, was still to come. Miranda smiled gleefully; maybe it would teach him to be more circumspect in future.

There were several messages waiting for her when Miranda got to work. Megan gave her the list, adding, 'Oh, and there was one rather strange call. A man rang to ask if you worked here, and when I said you did but that you weren't in, he just rang off without leaving any message or giving his name.'

It didn't take a million guesses to know who that could be. Deciding it might be wise to take a few precautions, Miranda said, 'Don't put any calls through to me unless you know who it is. And don't put any calls *at all* through from a man called Warren Hunter of Compass Consultants.'

'Had some aggro?' Megan asked sympathetically.

'You could say that.'

She settled down to do some work and was on the phone, in the middle of a delicate negotiation with an important contact, when the sound of raised voices out in the corridor intruded into her concentration. Miranda tried to ignore it, putting a finger against her ear as she listened to the voice on the other end. 'Well, yes, I'm sure the company will be happy to meet you over the choice of a car, but whether they will agree to——'

The door suddenly crashed back on its hinges and Warren Hunter burst in, with Megan hanging on to the back of his jacket in a useless attempt to try and stop him. Coming up to Miranda's desk, he put both hands on it and glared at her. 'I want a word with you.'

Miranda stared at him open-mouthed for a moment, then blinked and turned away to carry on with her phone call. 'As I was saying, I don't think the——'

But he reached out, wrenched the receiver from her hand and banged it down on the rest. 'You heard me; I want to talk to you.'

She glared at him, not in the least afraid. 'I have nothing further to say to you.'

'Well, that's where you're wrong—because you have some explaining to do.' He became aware that Megan was in the room and said peremptorily, 'Get out of here.'

Megan gasped and Miranda got angrily to her feet. 'How dare you order my secretary around?'

'All right, keep her here, for all I care. But I'm not leaving here until you explain that remark you made when you left the restaurant; about credit cards and what I use them to pay for,' he reminded her, his voice as cutting as steel.

'Shall I get Graham—and some of the men?' Megan added, after looking at the width of Warren's shoulders.

'No, I can handle this. It's OK, Megan, he's just a—a bad loser, that's all. Here.' She scribbled on a piece of paper. 'Call this man, apologise, and tell him I'll call him back very shortly.'

'Another fly being lured into your web?' Warren sneered as Megan went out.

'What I do is perfectly legal and provides a valuable service,' Miranda answered shortly.

'Tell that to the companies you pillage,' he said sarcastically, but then dismissed the subject with a curt movement of his hand. 'But that isn't why I came here. I want to know what the hell you were going on about in that restaurant.'

Miranda gave him a disgusted look. 'Don't try and play the innocent; you know very well what I meant.'

'Listen, lady, I don't know what you're hoping to gain, but if you think that you can get back at me by trying to ruin my reputation with a lot of lies, then you can——'

'Hah!' Miranda laughed in his face. 'It will give me great pleasure to blacken whatever shreds of reputation you have left. And they won't be lies, as you very well know. So don't think I won't, you louse!'

Straightening up, Warren took a swift stride round the desk and caught her wrist. 'I am getting extremely tired of you and your abuse,' he informed her with scarcely suppressed rage.

'Don't think you can browbeat me,' Miranda retorted defiantly. 'I'm not a push-over like Rosalind.'

'And am I supposed to know who Rosalind is?'

'If you don't you have a damn short memory,' she said furiously, her voice rising. 'Rosalind is my sister. Rosalind Leigh. Do you remember her now? The eighteen-year old university student you seduced. The girl you got pregnant. The girl you walked out on! The girl you——'

Catching hold of her shoulders, Warren shook her, just once, cutting her off in mid-tirade. 'What the hell are you talking about? I don't know any girl called Rosalind.'

'Liar!' Miranda spat the word at him like a whiplash. 'And if you don't take your hands off me I'll scream the place down.'

Staring at her face, seeing the intense fury in her eyes, Warren slowly removed his hands and stepped back. 'You'd better explain. Because you're making one hell of a mistake.'

'Nice try,' she sneered back at him. 'But this is one time when you're not going to just turn your back on all the hurt you've caused.'

'What hurt? For God's sake, woman, will you stop yelling and explain what you're talking about?'

Miranda hadn't realised that she'd been yelling, but his words made her aware that people might overhear and she stopped to draw breath, her face alive with anger, chest heaving. Lowering her voice almost to a vicious whisper, she said, 'Just how many girls do you seduce, that you forget them so easily?'

His jaw thrust forward and Warren reached out as if he was going to take hold of her again, but then he thought better of it and doubled his hand into a fist. 'I have never met anyone like you before and I hope I never do again. You're enough to try the patience of every saint in the Bible! I am *not* in the habit of seducing girls. I don't know any Rosalind Leigh. And I certainly don't walk out on my responsibilities.'

'No?' Miranda glared at him as she came out with her trump card. 'Then how come you paid for her to have an abortion?'

'What!' He stared at her in disbelief. 'You're out of your mind. I tell you I don't even know your sister. Did she tell you all this about me? Because if so——'

'No, she didn't. But I know you paid for the abortion because I saw your name at the clinic. It was on the form saying how the—the patient was going to pay. And you opted to pay by credit card. If you don't remember why don't you look at your credit statement?' she flashed at him.

'Maybe I'll do just that because I certainly——'
Warren broke off, his eyes widening. 'Wait a
minute. When was this?'

'Don't tell me you're actually starting to remember now?' Miranda said with heavy sarcasm.

He frowned angrily. 'Just answer the question;
when was this?'

'About six weeks ago—as if you didn't know.'

'My locker at a sports club I belong to was broken
into about that time and my wallet with all the credit
cards was stolen. The thief used them a few times;
maybe that was one of them.'

Miranda lifted her eyes heavenwards and laughed
in amazed disbelief. 'Do you really expect me to
swallow something as ridiculous as that?'

'Why not? You seem to expect me to believe that
I've seduced a girl I've never even met.'

'Lord, what a snivelling coward you are,'
Miranda said in scornful distaste.

His face hardening, Warren said acidly, 'I could
call you a few names too, but right now all I want
is to get to the bottom of this. Just what exactly
did your sister tell you about this man who seduced
her?'

'About you, you mean. She told me that you were
the director of a computer company and that you
were...' Miranda hesitated, then decided to leave
out the bit about his being good-looking and
sophisticated '...that you lived in London and were
very experienced.'

'And my name, did she tell you that?'

Miranda had to be honest. 'No, she didn't, she
said that she just wanted to forget that a louse like
you ever existed. But I saw your name on that form
the clinic had used when they booked Rosalind in,

so there's no use you trying to crawl out of this one. I——'

'And hasn't it yet occurred to you that she could have had this affair with a different man entirely—the man who stole my wallet?'

For a moment it brought Miranda up short, but then she dismissed the idea out of hand. 'There's an easy way to settle this; I'll phone Rosalind up tonight and ask her if it was you.'

'I thought you said she wanted to forget everything?'

'I'll make her tell me. I'll——'

'Oh, no, you won't.'

'So you're ready to admit it at last, are you?'

Giving her an exasperated look, Warren shoved his hands in his pockets as if afraid of putting them round her neck and strangling her. 'Don't you ever listen? I've never met your sister. But either you and she have concocted this whole thing up between you for some reason, or else she's made it up and you believe her. And there's no way I'm going to let you talk to her without me being there and finding out what this is all about.'

Miranda frowned. 'What do you mean?'

'I mean that you and I are going to go and see her—right now!'

'But that's ridiculous! I only have to phone her to confirm...'

Warren shook his head, the menacing expression on his face silencing her. 'Oh, no. I want to be there when you find out you're wrong, and then I'm going to make you grovel in the dirt when you say sorry to me.'

Miranda's heart skipped a beat as she imagined him carrying out his threat. For a moment she wondered if she could possibly be making a mistake, but then she rallied and said, 'You worm! You're not going to wriggle out of this one so easily.'

'So let's go and see who's right, shall we? My car's outside and I want this settled now.'

Miranda laughed. 'Well, that's impossible. Rosalind isn't at university here; she's in York, as you very well know.'

His brows drew into a momentary frown, but then Warren shrugged. 'OK, so we'll go to York.'

He turned as if to go to the door but Miranda said, 'Don't think you can con me. I know I'm right.'

'So then you'll have the satisfaction of rubbing my nose in the dirt, won't you?'

He looked at her as he said it, his eyebrows raised mockingly, and his confidence shook her own again, but she said, 'If you think I'm going anywhere with you, you're crazy.'

He opened the door. 'All right. I'll go and find her myself.'

'No!' Miranda ran forward and grabbed hold of his arm. 'You're just making empty threats. I . . .' She paused, searching his face for some sign that he was bluffing and finding none. 'If you think I'm going to let you hurt her again after all she's been through——'

'Then you'd better come with me, hadn't you?'

Miranda stared into his strong, implacable face and recognised an iron will. 'You snake!'

'You,' he grated, 'are going to call me one name too many. Are you coming?'

'All right. Yes. Wait a minute.' Going to the cupboard in the corner she took out her coat and put it on, found a pair of gloves and picked up her bag.

'Ready?' Warren asked impatiently.

She gave him a withering look and swept past him into the main office. Megan and the other girls looked up with fascinated curiosity. 'Megan, will you tell Graham I won't be able to make dinner tonight?' Leaning forward she picked up a notepad and began to write on it, putting down where she was going and who with. 'An envelope, please.' She was aware of Warren's growing impatience but didn't hurry. 'If I'm not in to work by noon tomorrow give this to Graham and tell him to act on it, will you?' She glared at Warren. 'It tells him exactly where I'm going.' Her eyes added, So you needn't think you can try anything underhand.

He read the message all right, but his lip merely curled in disdain. 'Are you finally ready now?'

Her eyes shot fire at him but she nodded. 'Yes.' And walked ahead of him to the main door, but had just reached it when she said, 'Oh, my gloves.' and ran back to the desk. But as well as picking up her gloves she also grabbed up a portable phone that she'd seen lying there and shoved it into her bag. Then hurried back to join him.

His car was a red Lotus, long, lean and powerful. Completely wrong for a traffic-choked city, but just the car to attract young girls, Miranda thought savagely. He opened the door for her but Miranda, realising that she was going to show a lot of leg, said coldly, 'I can manage, thanks.'

'Suit yourself.' Warren went round the other side and got in.

The car was so low that Miranda felt as if she was sitting on the ground, but it was far more comfortable than she'd expected. Which was just as well if they were going all the way to York. Warren handled the car with expert ease, and was at home in London, ducking down side streets to avoid the major traffic jams and soon heading north to pick up the motorway. As they drove, Miranda began to wonder what on earth she was doing there, sitting beside this man who had done such harm to her sister. She was sure that it was just going to be a wild-goose chase that would inevitably end with upsetting Rosalind all over again. So why had she allowed herself to be coerced into it?

She stirred uneasily and raised her hands to put up the collar of her coat, lifting her hair out from under it. Glancing at her, Warren said, 'Cold?' and reached out to turn up the heater.

Leaning back against the head-rest, Miranda stole a look at his profile. She had looked at him before, of course, but taken in only the outward signs that she had been expecting to see; the self-confidence and handsomeness that had so attracted Rosalind. But that verbal duel in her office had shown her that there was steel below the surface, and a dominant will-power that somehow didn't fit the Casanova figure that she'd expected. It just didn't seem right. And it was this shadow of doubt, a moment's terrifying fear that she might be wrong, that had led her to come with him.

But then Miranda remembered Rosalind saying that he was the type of man that Miranda herself might have gone for. Well, that was true enough; if she hadn't known Warren's history she might well have fancied him. And he wasn't married, he was free to... Her mind froze. Free to seduce young girls like Rosalind. Which must make him some kind of pervert. And she had been stupid enough to agree to go on this journey with him. The thought sent such a strong tremor of trepidation running through her that Warren noticed.

'Still cold? I'm afraid I can't turn the heater up any higher.'

'No, it's OK.'

Cursing herself for being a fool, Miranda knew that she had to find out about Warren Hunter one way or another, and she certainly didn't intend to wait until they got to York and found Rosalind. Thank goodness she'd had the forethought to grab the portable phone. Now all she had to do was create a chance to use it without Warren knowing. They reached the motorway as dusk fell and he put his foot down, zipping confidently through the traffic.

'Could you stop at the next service station?'

He nodded but then gave her a quick glance, but could see little of her face in the dim light. After a moment, he said, 'How long have you been working for the headhunters?'

'Executive searchers,' Miranda corrected automatically, then added, 'Nearly eighteen months.'

'What's the attraction?'

She considered not answering him—she certainly didn't feel like having a conversation—but the atmosphere was tense enough, so she said, 'It's challenging work and it pays well.'

'And you get to meet such interesting people,' he said on a derisive laugh. 'You sound like a candidate in a beauty contest, repeating something parrot fashion. Tell me, don't you ever wonder what effect your—work——' his lip curled '—has on the employers you steal personnel from?'

'The people don't have to leave,' Miranda pointed out. 'A lot of them use our approach as a lever to get more money from their current bosses. And as for the others,' she shrugged, 'I suppose it's something like a marriage bureau; we find employers and employees who are compatible.'

Warren gave a harsh laugh. 'What a way to look on such a low occupation as yours.'

'Are you saying that you wouldn't use headhunters if you were looking for a new employee?' Miranda retorted, goaded into arguing the issue.

'Certainly not. I prefer to recruit my own staff.'

Well, you'll certainly be doing that a lot sooner than you envisage, she thought with satisfaction.

But she didn't speak and Warren said, 'I suppose the fact that another company was looking for someone with Jonathan Carter's qualifications gave you an ideal opportunity to try to get back at me?'

'Obviously.'

'But you must have done some detective work to find out about my company and employees?'

'Of course. It's part of my job.'

'I find that thoroughly abhorrent,' he said shortly. 'To have vultures like you digging into my business makes my flesh creep.'

'Anyone who starts a business lays himself open for inspection,' Miranda returned. 'There are a whole lot of people who look into companies: the inland revenue, auditors——'

'Those are to be expected; they're hardly scavenging predators like you.'

Realising that they were only heading for another argument, Miranda gestured towards the side of the road. 'We just passed a sign for a service station.'

'Yes, I saw it.'

Cutting through the lanes of traffic, he pulled off the motorway and parked in front of the service area. It was completely dark now and the air struck very cold as Miranda got out of the car. She shivered, pulling her coat close around her against the cutting wind. Warren followed her as she hurried across to the brightly lit entrance, which was a nuisance; she'd hoped he would stay in the car. But evidently he didn't trust her because he watched her until she went into the ladies' cloakroom.

Luckily Miranda's handbag was the organiser type and contained her address book. She looked up Rosalind's number and called it, hoping that there would be someone in the lodging house where Rosalind had her digs. The number rang and rang and she was on the point of giving up when somebody finally answered. The line was terrible, which was only to be expected when she was stuck inside a concrete block. Moving as near to the door as possible, Miranda had to yell to make herself heard. 'Can you get Rosalind Leigh for me, please?'

'I'm not sure she's in. Hang on.' The words were almost lost in the static.

Another long wait as Miranda tapped her foot impatiently; maybe she would have done better to wait until they were further up the motorway, but she just had to know.

'Hello? Rosalind Leigh here.'

'Oh, thank goodness. Roz, it's Miranda.'

'Who? I can't hear.'

The door was screened outside by an arch. Miranda took a chance and went through the door to stand in its shelter. 'Is that better? It's Miranda.'

'Oh, yes. Is anything the matter?'

'Roz, this is most important. You have *got* to tell me the name of the man. You know who.'

'I can't.' Rosalind's voice rose in distress. 'I told you, I——'

Aware of the passing of time, Miranda said desperately, 'Is his name Warren Hunter?'

Even over the bad line she heard her sister gasp. 'How did you find out? I——'

A hand grabbed hold of Miranda's collar and yanked her out into the open, pulled her round so that Warren could see the phone in her hand. 'Of all the dirty tricks. I thought we agreed to face your sister together?'

Miranda pushed down the aerial and glared back at him. 'No, you *ordered* me not to phone her; I certainly didn't make any promise not to.'

'And did you reach her?'

'Yes, I did.'

He looked at the triumphant anger in her hazel eyes and turned away.

'Aren't you going to ask me what she said?' Miranda demanded, catching his sleeve.

'I don't have to; it's written all over your face.'

'So you can stop lying, then, and end this farce of a journey.'

He looked down at her, his lips set into a thin line, his face cold. 'Now there's even more reason to go to York, because your sister is the one who's lying her head off—and I'm going to find out why.'

Turning, he strode out of the building and, after a moment's surprise, Miranda ran after him. He got back in the car and for a horrible moment she thought he was going to drive away without her, but then he reached across and unlocked the car from the inside. She got in and stared at his set profile. If Rosalind hadn't given herself away like that she could almost have believed him. But it was impossible for there to be two people with such an unusual name and both directors of a computer company; that was stretching coincidence too far. And it also knocked to pieces his suggestion that someone might have used his stolen credit card, because Rosalind had met him back in the summer and his card had only been stolen a few weeks ago.

He's crazy, Miranda decided, to go on with this stupid charade. What on earth does he think he has to gain by it? They resumed the journey and she looked at the man sitting beside her in growing unease. Maybe she would have done better to stay behind at the service station. If he could treat Rosalind so brutally then heaven only knew what he might do to her. As a safeguard she said firmly, 'They know at the office that I'm with you and where I'm going, remember.'

He threw her a moody look, but saw the way that she had drawn into the corner of her seat and his eyebrows rose in surprise. 'Good lord, you're not afraid of me, are you? I assure you, lady, that you're absolutely safe from me—I wouldn't touch you if you were the last woman left on earth!'

Which should have been a comforting remark but definitely wasn't. Miranda glared at him but settled back in her seat more comfortably. The miles sped by as the powerful car headed further north. The air grew colder and Miranda could see frost on the ground and on the roofs of houses. They stopped at another service station to fill up with petrol and frost patterns gathered on the windscreen in just that short time.

When Warren got back in the car he turned on the radio and they heard the forecast of snow in the north on the weather report. As Miranda listened she wished heartily that Rosalind could have chosen Cambridge or Oxford to go to university instead of somewhere so far away. There were hold-ups on the approach to the city and it was almost eight o'clock before they reached York, then Miranda wasn't sure of the way to Rosalind's digs and they had to ask so it was almost eight-thirty before they finally pulled up outside the house.

As Warren switched off the engine she turned to him. 'If you upset Rosalind, I'll kill you,' she threatened. 'She's gone through enough. I don't know what you're trying to prove by this game you're playing but——'

'My innocence,' Warren cut in forcefully. 'And your crass stupidity. Come on, let's get this over with.'

He got out of the car and locked it, then strode down the path to the front door and hammered on the knocker. One of the students came to open it and he strode past him with Miranda close on his heels. 'Which is her room?'

'Upstairs. No, let me go first.'

He hesitated, then stepped aside. Rosalind's room was on the second floor. Miranda ran up the worn-carpeted stairs and knocked.

'Door's open. Come in.'

Miranda reached out to the knob, but hesitated uncertainly, her heart thumping, worried at what this confrontation might do to her sister.

'What are you waiting for?' Warren demanded tauntingly. 'Afraid of being shown up for a fool?'

She glowered at him and opened the door.

Rosalind was sitting at a table, working on an essay, and jumped up in surprise when she saw who it was. 'Miranda! What are you doing here? And why did you make that phone call? How did you——?' She broke off as Warren followed Miranda into the room. 'Oh, sorry, I didn't realise you had someone with you.' She looked at Warren with politely masked curiosity, but there was no other reaction, no cry of hatred or lost love, no look of despair, or even embarrassment.

Miranda looked into her sister's face and knew that she had made the most ghastly mistake. At that moment she would gladly have been struck into oblivion by a merciful bolt of lightning, anything rather than have to face Warren again.

'Hello.' Rosalind looked at Warren and smiled. 'Do come in, both of you. I'm afraid the place isn't very tidy.' She went to straighten up the settee but saw Miranda's face and said, 'Is anything the matter?'

Her voice sounding terribly unnatural even to her own ears, Miranda said, 'I take it you haven't met this man before?'

Rosalind looked mystified. 'Why, no. Did you think I had?'

Weakly Miranda said, 'Well, yes, I thought you might have done. You see, his name is Warren Hunter.'

Rosalind's mouth dropped open and she goggled at them both. 'But he isn't . . . He isn't the man I—I told you about.'

'You're quite sure?' Miranda asked in futile despair.

'Of course I'm sure. I should know, shouldn't I?' There was a moment of awful silence until Rosalind, completely bewildered, said, 'Is that why you rang me?'

'Yes.' Grasping at waterlogged straws, Miranda said accusingly, 'You said his name was Warren Hunter.'

'No, I didn't!'

'Well, not exactly, no. But when I asked you if his name was Warren Hunter, you asked me how I'd found out.'

'Yes, I know that,' Rosalind retorted. 'But...' she hesitated '...oh, I suppose I'll have to tell you. The man—his name is Warren-Hunter, but that's his surname; his full name is Piers Warren-Hunter. I thought you'd just found out his surname.'

'What! Good grief, I should have guessed.' The words came from Warren and they both turned to stare at him. 'He's probably a distant connection of mine,' he explained. 'Warren is a very common name in my family; it's a tradition going back a long way to pass the name down to the eldest son. But about a hundred years or so ago one of the side branches adopted it into their surname.'

Miranda's legs suddenly lost their strength and she tottered to a chair and sank in it. She put her head in her hands, unable to look either of them in the face. Oh, lord, she'd made such a hash of things. He'll kill me, she thought, and he'll have every right.

'But I don't understand,' she heard Rosalind saying to Warren. 'Surely you told Miranda that— that you didn't know me?'

'I did, but she wouldn't listen. She was convinced she was right. Weren't you, Miranda?'

He waited for her to answer and she stole a glance at him but couldn't bear the look of smug satisfaction on his face and hastily turned away again.

'That's why I insisted that we come here to see you,' Warren went on. 'To put the record straight.'

'But I still don't understand how Miranda found you in the first place. I didn't tell her the name of—of——'

'Of your boyfriend,' Warren said helpfully. 'Naturally not. If I were you I'd tell her as little as possible about my private affairs as well. Tell me, does she always charge into things like the proverbial bull at a gate?' Without waiting for Rosalind to answer, he went on, 'It seems she saw the name Warren-Hunter on a form at the clinic where you were a patient, and you told her your boyfriend was in computers so she did some scouting around and came up with me. And that, of course, was as far as she bothered to look.'

'That isn't true.' Miranda lifted her head to contradict him, but saw the steely look in his eyes and lowered it again.

'As I was saying,' Warren went on, 'your sister was so hell-bent on getting even with your boyfriend that she tried to do the dirty on me by using her company to suborn one of my employees, but luckily for me—and for her as it turns out—it didn't work.'

Miranda's face tightened with horror as she remembered the other seven employees that she *had* succeeded with and who were due to hand in their collective notice in just a few days' time. Oh, no!

she groaned inwardly. *When he finds out he really will kill me!*

'You did that for me?' Warren raised his eyebrows as Rosalind saw only what her sister had tried to do for her and went to kneel beside Miranda.

Miranda took her hand and gave her a wan little smile. 'I was so mad that you'd been treated so badly. I thought I'd try and teach him a lesson. Only the whole thing has gone so horribly wrong.'

'Serves you damn well right for going through with such a stupid idea,' Warren put in.

She shot him an angry look under her lashes. The man had a right to his triumph, but there was just so much she could take. Then she remembered his threat to make her grovel and it occurred to her that he was expecting an apology, and an abject one at that. Her heart sank all over again; what was the use of apologising now when he still didn't know the half of it?

'But thanks, anyway,' Rosalind said and gave her a hug.

'Are you over it now?'

Rosalind's face shadowed for a moment, but then she shrugged. 'As much as I'll ever be, I suppose. I've been taking your advice to keep busy; there's hardly an activity in the university that I haven't joined.'

'That's great.' Miranda stood up reluctantly. 'I suppose we'd better go.'

'Already?' The disappointment was plain in Rosalind's voice.

Warren looked from one to the other of them, the two girls so much alike with their fair hair and slim figures, but Rosalind so obviously the younger and much more vulnerable sister. 'I'm not going anywhere until I've eaten,' he said firmly. 'Thanks to your wildcat schemes I've had hardly anything today.'

Remembering the way he'd been too angry to eat at the restaurant at lunchtime, a flush of guilt filled Miranda's cheeks and she raised an unsteady hand to cover it.

'Is there a take-away or something near here?' Warren asked Rosalind.

'There's a really good Chinese on the main road. I'll go and get some, shall I?'

'No, I'll go.' Warren gave a sardonic smile. 'I'm sure you two have a lot to talk about—and maybe you'll even get your facts right this time.'

She deserved that, that and much more, Miranda realised. She stood aside as Rosalind gave him directions, but when he turned to her and said, 'What would you like to eat?' she shook her head.

'I—I'm not hungry, thanks.'

He gave her an intent look, noting her unhappy face, and didn't argue. 'I'll be back shortly.'

When he'd gone Miranda slumped into a chair again and said, 'Oh, God, Roz, I've made the most dreadful mistake.'

'Yes, I know; he told me.'

'No, you don't, it's much worse than that. I wanted to ruin him, you see, the same way he ruined your life. Only not Warren, this other man—your boyfriend, only I thought it was Warren. Oh, hell, you know what I mean.' She saw that Rosalind was grinning, and snapped, 'It isn't funny. He thinks I only tried to lure one person away from his company but there were——' She stopped abruptly. This was her problem and she had no right to thrust it on to Rosalind, who had enough problems of her own. 'It doesn't matter. I'll sort it out.'

Agitatedly she got up and went to the window. There was an electric fire and a radiator in the room and it was warm enough, but the cold wind blowing outside was strong enough to lift the thin curtain. 'This man—Piers Warren-Hunter, was he really in computers?'

'Yes, he was one of the owners of a shop that sold them.'

Which was a world away from what Warren did, Miranda realised with a heavy sigh, although she supposed the description still fitted. She turned back to Rosalind. 'Are you really OK?'

'Yes. Aren't you going to tell me what you were going to say?'

Miranda shook her head and gave a lop-sided smile. 'I suppose I'm like you; can't bring myself to admit my mistakes.'

'When did you meet him; Warren Hunter?'

Miranda sighed. 'At one o'clock this afternoon.' Without mentioning the other employees, she told Rosalind the rest of the story.

'Wow, no wonder he's so furious with you,' Rosalind said in awe when she'd finished. 'What do you think he'll do—go to your boss and try and get you sacked or something?'

Miranda hadn't thought of that one. Graham wouldn't be at all pleased, of course; in fact he'd probably be stunned, but she was sure that he wouldn't sack her when she explained the circumstances. But it was still a very unpleasant thought. 'I don't know; he might. He said—he said that he was going to make me grovel.'

Rosalind stared at her, then said rather hollowly, 'He looks the kind of man who means what he says.'

The front doorbell sounded down below as Miranda raised her eyes to meet her sister's. 'Yes,' she agreed unhappily. 'I'm very much afraid he does.'

CHAPTER THREE

THERE was a thin coating of snow on the shoulders of Warren's jacket when he came back into Rosalind's room, carrying the spicy-smelling bag of Chinese food.

'It's getting extremely wintry out there,' he remarked.

He glanced at Miranda but she had gone over to the table and was looking blindly down at Rosalind's essay. It was impossible to distance herself from Warren physically in the small room, but she was trying to mentally distance herself from the situation, putting off the moment when she would have to confess the whole truth.

'I'll get some plates. Perhaps you could clear that table for me, Miranda?' Rosalind said tactfully.

Miranda did so but was unnecessarily fussy about stacking the books tidily, so that the other two were ready to sit down to eat before she'd finished. Warren held a chair for Rosalind then stood by the table, waiting. 'Are you going to sit down or do we eat standing up?' he demanded impatiently.

Reluctantly she came over and took the chair he offered, but edged it further away from him. Warren's lips twisted in ironic amusement but he made no comment.

He had brought enough food for her as well, but Miranda couldn't eat. The dread of his reaction when she finally told him just what she'd done tightened her throat so that she could hardly swallow. But Warren had also brought a bottle of wine and she drank her glass down greedily, hoping that it would serve not only to ease the tension but to give her some badly needed courage. She sat silently in her chair, her eyes fixed on her plate and with nothing to say, but Warren chatted to Rosalind easily enough, asking her about her college course and carefully refraining from mentioning the reason for their visit. The younger girl responded somewhat reluctantly at first but he soon had her laughing, and drew her out until Rosalind was talking animatedly, her face flushed and eager. So he had charm as well, did he? Miranda thought morosely. And she couldn't help wondering what the outcome would have been if Rosalind had had an affair with Warren instead of his distant relation.

As if feeling her eyes on him, Warren turned towards her but Miranda looked quickly away, pushing a few beansprouts round her plate. Seeing that her glass was empty, he picked up the bottle of wine and refilled it. She murmured a word of thanks and reached out for it, but as she glanced up found that he was watching her. His eyes held hers compellingly for a long moment, letting her see the contemptuous amusement in their grey depths.

'Not hungry?' he asked derisively. 'Now what can have spoiled your appetite, I wonder?'

A thought occurred to her and Miranda said stiltedly, 'I owe you for the food. And for—for the meal in the restaurant at lunchtime.'

'This is my treat,' Warren replied. 'But yes, you do owe me for lunch——' he paused deliberately '—and for a whole lot more. But you don't have to worry; I won't ask you to pay by credit card.'

He let that sink in, turning away to continue eating, but as soon as he'd finished his meal he stood up and went over to the window.

'The snow is coming down more heavily. Would you mind if we put the radio on to get a weather forecast?' he asked Rosalind.

'Of course not. I'll make some coffee.'

Warren tuned into a local radio station and it wasn't long before they got a weather report of heavy snow and strong winds for the rest of the night. 'We'd better get going,' Warren decided. But almost immediately there was a traffic warning of a big jam on the main road leading from the city due to a lorry overturning and spilling a dangerous load.

'There are already long tail-backs and the road isn't expected to be opened for at least two hours,' the announcer reported.

'Is there an alternative route?' Warren asked Rosalind.

'There's another main road but that will probably be jammed with traffic, too, and it's a long way round. But there's a lesser road which is easy to reach from this side of York and goes right down to the motorway. It's only a B road and tends to wind rather a lot but——'

'Sounds fine,' Warren cut in. 'I'll get my road map and perhaps you could show it to me.'

As soon as he'd left them to go down to the car, Rosalind turned eagerly to Miranda. 'Why don't you stay here tonight and go back to London by train tomorrow? Then you won't have Warren gloating over you the whole way back.'

It was an incredibly tempting suggestion. For a few moments Miranda almost succumbed, thinking that she could give Warren the bad news about his other employees by letter, but then she squared her shoulders and shook her head. 'I would love to, I really would, but I have to see this through.'

Footsteps sounded on the stairs and Warren came in. He looked at the two of them standing so close together, and his left eyebrow rose as Miranda immediately moved away. He spread the map on the table and Rosalind pointed out the alternative route.

'Mm, it's longer, but as you say it should cut out the worst of the jams. We'd better leave now before the weather worsens.' He turned to Miranda and added grimly, 'And you're coming with me, so don't get any ideas about staying behind.'

Rosalind made a sound of protest but Miranda held up her hand, silencing her. 'I had no intention of staying here,' she told him steadily.

His brows rose in disbelief but Miranda put on her coat then went over to say goodbye to Rosalind. 'Take care of yourself, you hear me?'

'I will. And thanks for—for caring about me so much.' She glanced uneasily at Warren. 'Are you sure you'll be OK?'

'Yes, of course. I'll give you a ring tomorrow evening.' The two girls hugged each other tightly for a moment and then Miranda resolutely turned and strode out of the room without waiting for Warren to follow her.

The snow was falling so thickly that there was already a coating of white over the cars in the street. Miranda put up the collar of her coat against the wind as she waited for Warren to unlock the Lotus. Once inside he put the map book in her hands. 'Here, we want the B1228.'

The streets were well lit but the orange glow of the lamps had a ghostly effect in the snow. There were other cars going along, enough to keep the roads clear, and they made quite good progress to the outskirts of the city where they came to a big roundabout and picked up the minor road. Miranda had been concentrating on following the direction signs, but once they were on the lesser road she sat back, knowing that they had to stay on it for several miles before they reached the motorway.

This must be the time, she realised. She had to tell him now before they reached the motorway and Warren had to concentrate entirely on his driving. It was a lonely, open road through flat fields and there were no more street lights and very few houses. Miranda was grateful for the darkness; she didn't want to see his face when she told him. The Lotus purred along, taking the bad conditions in its stride, the one windscreen wiper swinging rhythmically from side to side. The interior of the car was warm and comfortable now and Warren sat relaxed in his seat, as capable as the car of dealing with the snow. Glancing across at her he said, 'Are we going to sit in frigid silence again all the way back?'

It was as if he'd deliberately given her an opening. Clearing her throat Miranda said, 'As a matter of fact there is something I want to say to you.'

'Don't tell me I'm actually going to get an apology from you?' he said scathingly.

'No, not yet.' She paused, desperately seeking the words to soften the blow, but knowing that there weren't any.

Mistaking her hesitation, Warren said in chauvinistic amusement, 'You just can't bring yourself to admit that you made a mistake, can you? You're a poor loser, just like all women; they always hate to admit that they're in the wrong.'

'You sound as if you have a lot of experience with women,' Miranda remarked, making it sound like an accusation.

'Some,' he admitted. 'Well? I'm still waiting for your apology,' he pointed out.

Miranda felt a flash of hatred at his malevolent tone, but, realising how quickly it was going to change to dismay and anger, gathered up her courage and said, 'There's something I haven't yet told you.'

'Oh, really.' Warren slowed down as they came to a crossroads. 'Which way?'

'What? Oh, straight ahead,' Miranda answered with only a glance at the increasingly snow-compacted windscreen. 'Stay on this road. It—it was about your company. You see, Jonathan Carter wasn't the only one of your employees that I headhunted.'

She had his full attention now. 'And were you successful?'

'Yes.'

He glanced at the road then back at her. 'All right; who is it?'

Her hands balled into tight fists, her heart thumping, Miranda managed to say, 'Actually there was more than one.'

Warren's mouth set into grim lines. 'How many?' For a moment she couldn't answer and he said impatiently, 'Don't stop now. How many?'

Taking a deep breath, Miranda said, 'Seven.'

'*What?*' Warren jammed his foot on the brake, too amazed and angry to drive. But he must have hit a patch of frozen snow because the car skidded across the road, swinging towards the edge, then suddenly slewed over on to the driver's side as they went into a ditch.

Miranda cried out in alarm and grabbed hold of his arm as she fell against him. Warren swore explosively into the sudden silence as the engine stalled. 'My God, this is all I need.' He turned his head towards her. 'Are you all right?'

'Yes.'

'Then you don't damn well deserve to be.'

Shaken out of one fear by a greater one, Miranda retorted, 'Well, it's no thanks to you if I am. It was you who landed us in this ditch.' She groped for the catch of her safety strap and released it but fell across Warren's lap.

'Don't mind me,' he said sarcastically.

'I won't. Lift me up so I can open my door.' He did so, none too gently, and Miranda managed to struggle out of the car and on to the road. It was bitterly cold; hastily Miranda did up her coat and thanked her stars that she was wearing boots. 'Can you pass up my gloves and bag?'

Warren gave her a look that was even more freezing than the weather, but passed up her things, the map book, a big torch, and his briefcase, before clambering out of the car himself. Putting up the collar of his jacket, he walked round it, then shook his head. 'It's hopeless; we'll have to get someone to tow it out.' He looked all round but there were no houses, no lights anywhere. 'We'll just have to walk until we find a phone, though God knows how long it will take for anyone to get out here with a tow truck in these conditions.' He gave her a murderous look. 'You certainly couldn't have picked a better spot to make your charming little admission.'

'It isn't my fault you're such a rotten driver,' Miranda retorted, driven into childishness by guilt.

Warren gave her a disgusted look, picked up his briefcase and started to stride off down the road, the beam of the torch lighting the way.

'You might wait for me,' Miranda panted as she hurried to catch him up.

'If you can't keep up, go and wait in the car,' he answered unfeelingly.

'And freeze to death? No way.'

Like most men who drove everywhere by car, in London anyway, Warren had no overcoat and was wearing only a thin shirt under his suit jacket. But he didn't seem to feel the cold too much. Probably it was anger that kept him warm because he snapped out, 'So who are these seven people that you've coerced to leave my company?'

He had to raise his voice against the wind but Miranda had no difficulty in hearing. 'Can't it wait until we——?'

'I want to know *now*.'

Reluctantly she told him, tilting her head high because he was so much taller, her heart sinking as his face became grimmer with each name. 'What— what are you going to do?' she faltered as she came to the end of the list.

'When are they due to leave?'

'They are all going to hand in their notice on the first of December.'

'Oh, nice. The sort of touch only you could think up,' Warren remarked harshly. 'I'll just have to phone each of them and...' He broke off. 'Lord, what fools we are; you've got a phone in your bag.'

'What? Oh, yes, of course.' Her fingers were so cold, even with gloves on, that Miranda had difficulty unzipping her bag, and then almost dropped the phone when she fished it out.

'Careful.' Warren grabbed it and pulled out the aerial.

'Who are you going to call?'

'The police. I'll get them to phone the nearest garage.'

Turning her back against the wind, Miranda huddled into her coat as she waited, her hair blowing across her face, snow settling on her dark lashes.

Warren held the phone against his ear, struggling to hear. 'I can't seem to get anything.' He tried again, then reached out an arm and pulled her towards him, making a cave with their bodies against the noise of the wind. 'No, still nothing,' he said in exasperation.

'There should be a little light that comes on when you switch it on,' Miranda said helpfully. 'It was OK when I . . .' She stopped suddenly, a ghastly thought entering her brain.

'Well?' Warren saw her face and gave her a dangerous look. 'You'd better tell me.'

'I think I must have forgotten to turn it off after I called Rosalind. The battery must be dead.'

'And don't tell me—you didn't think to bring a spare unit,' he said heavily.

'No. Why should I? I only grabbed the phone at the last minute because I wasn't happy about travelling across half the country with a man like you. How was I to know you were going to drive into a ditch?'

Giving her a glowering look, Warren gritted his teeth as he said feelingly, 'Lady, you didn't need the phone—I did! Any man who's stupid enough to get within a mile of you needs police protection.'

Thrusting the useless gadget at her, Warren strode on again, head bent against the wind. The snow seemed to get worse as they trudged on so that a couple of times they almost strayed from the road. Miranda's hair was completely wet now and her teeth were chattering; she was frozen even with her coat and could only imagine how Warren must be feeling.

He stopped for a moment and searched the darkness, wiping the snow from his face. 'We should have reached a village by now; it was marked on the map.' But there was nothing in sight and they plodded on again.

Miranda was beginning to feel very tired but determination not to give Warren another reason to yell at her kept her going, but it was almost half a mile further on before they came to a crossroads with a signpost. 'At last!' Warren lifted the torch to see the sign but had to reach up and brush away the snow before they could read it. He stared at it in perplexity. 'But that says that the B1228 is over to our right. But it can't be unless . . .' He stopped and swung to face her, the beam of the torch shining in her face. 'Good grief! Can't you get anything right? You've sent us in the wrong direction. We're miles from the road we wanted!'

'But we can't be. You must have misread it.' Grabbing the torch from him, Miranda swung it back on the sign and saw with a sick feeling of despair that he was right. 'Oh, no!'

'Of all the useless, vindictive, stupid——'

'Shut up! I'm just about sick and tired of you yelling at me,' Miranda shouted back, exhaustion snapping the thin thread of her temper. 'Anyone can make a mistake, for heaven's sake.'

'A mistake! Is that what you call this fiasco? Let me tell you——'

'No, let me tell you for once. You're a great overbearing, chauvinistic, intolerant rat. And I...' She stopped, suddenly realising that they were standing in the middle of the road and having a shouting match in a blizzard. 'Oh, what's the use?' Throwing the torch at him, she turned on her heel and strode down the road to the left.

Neatly fielding the torch, Warren shouted, 'Where do you think you're going?'

'Anywhere so long as it's not with you!'

'You're crazy, you'll get lost. Come back here.'

'Don't you dare order me around,' Miranda yelled back over her shoulder. 'And you can stop coming after me because I——' She felt the ground fall away under her feet and too late turned to look where she was going. She slid gracefully down a steep bank and splashed into the freezing cold water of a weed-covered river.

Her scream of terror cut through the snow-storm like a knife, but the next moment Warren was there, throwing himself on the ground and reaching down to grab her hand. 'All right, I've got you. Don't panic.' Taking hold of her other hand, he tried to pull her out, but after a few minutes said, 'It's too steep for me to drag you out; I can't get any purchase in the snow. Can you try and climb up my arms until I can lift you?'

He spoke calmly, steadily, and his voice did a lot to still Miranda's terror. 'Yes. Yes, all right.' She tried but the weight of her coat pulled her down. 'I'll have to take my coat off.'

'OK. One arm at a time. Don't worry; I won't let you go.'

The shock of the cold water had got to her and Miranda's whole body shook as she struggled to take off the heavy coat. She let it go to the bottom of the river with her bag, too scared to care. Using all that was left of her strength, she managed to inch herself up Warren's arms until he could put his hands under her arms and slowly drag her back with him. Afterwards Miranda lay on the ground, gasping for breath, just overwhelmingly grateful to be out of the water.

'Come on, you must get up. You'll freeze in those wet clothes.

'I—I can't.' Miranda spoke through teeth that rattled like gunfire in her head.

'Yes, you can. Come on.' Warren hoisted her to her feet and took off his jacket. 'Here, put this on.'

'But you——'

'Do as you're told,' he said roughly, and pushed her arms into the sleeves. 'Now, you have to walk.'

Putting his arm round her, Warren marched her along. Miranda didn't attempt to look where they were going, she just concentrated on putting one foot in front of the other. She was aware of Warren talking to her, encouraging her, but her boots were full of water and sloshed as she walked. And she was so cold, so cold.

'We have to get help,' she mumbled.

'I know. We will. Soon, now; we just have to keep going.'

She lost track of time and distance and didn't know how far they'd gone when Warren suddenly stopped and exclaimed. 'There are some buildings over there by the river.'

Oh, thank God! Miranda thought gratefully and tried to open her eyes. 'I can't see anything.'

'Over there. Come on, not far now.' Almost dragging her along, Warren turned off the road towards the snow-covered buildings, then gave a cry of disappointment. 'They're boats. But they're still shelter.' He looked at Miranda worriedly, then leaned her against a tree. 'Miranda! Open your eyes, look at me.' She did so and saw the look of blue, pinched cold in his face. 'That's it. Good girl. Now I'm going to find some shelter for us. You mustn't go to sleep. Do you understand?' She managed to nod and he grinned. 'Good. You can be thinking of all the names you want to call me until I get back. OK?' She managed to nod again and this time attempted a travesty of his grin. An amazed look came into his eyes and Warren shook his head. 'Lady, you are something else.'

He left her and Miranda pulled his jacket closer around her, although now it was as sodden as the rest of her clothes. She concentrated on staying standing up and thought of all the hot things she could think of: huge log fires, curry, the sun . . .

It seemed like ages, but Warren was back in just a few minutes. He took one look at her face and picked her up to carry her along the riverbank to the boat he'd picked out, lifting her on board and under the canopy. There was an immediate relief from the wind, but Miranda hardly noticed as he set her down while he broke open the door to the cabin, kicking in the lock.

The next hour only slowly resolved itself into different actions which she dimly felt. Her outer clothes were stripped off her and she was wrapped in a blanket, then rubbed vigorously until she began to protest. Then Warren left her and she gratefully slumped down where she sat and fell asleep, but he was soon back and carried her to the tiny shower-room opening off the main cabin, where he made her stand under the hot water until feeling and sensation slowly crept back and she became aware of what was happening. Warren was still wearing his clothes but was getting as soaked by the shower as she was.

'Can you manage by yourself now?'

She nodded. 'Yes.'

'All right. Dry yourself with the blanket while I go and see if I can warm the place up a bit and find some dry clothes.'

When he came back Warren was wearing an old sweater and a pair of jeans that were too small for him, his bare feet poking out at the bottom. He grinned when he saw her look him over. 'That's nothing; see what I've got for you.' And he produced an old sweat-shirt with a sailing ship on it and a pair of paint-stained overalls.

'If they're dry then they're the most gorgeous clothes I've ever seen,' Miranda told him fervently.

He laughed. 'The boat should start warming up soon; they've got central heating and I managed to get it going. Now I'll see if I can make a hot drink.'

'Oh, please,' she said longingly. Outwardly she was warm again now, but inside she still felt as if her bones were frozen.

She put on the smelly clothes, only now realising that Warren must have undressed her as well as holding her under the shower. Finding that she had mixed feelings about that, Miranda pushed them aside; right now all she wanted to think about was getting warm. There was carpet on the floor of the cabin but her feet were cold, so she started pulling out drawers, but couldn't find anything to wear.

'The owners must have taken most of their stuff away for the winter,' Warren remarked, coming in and finding her kneeling on the floor. 'Here, try this.'

He handed her a steaming mug of coffee that, when Miranda went to drink it, smelt strongly of brandy. She raised her eyebrows. 'Cognac?'

'I always a carry a small flask around in my briefcase,' Warren explained.

He sat beside her on the upholstered seat and for a while they were both content just to sit and drink, but presently Miranda said, 'How about you; are you warm enough? Did you have a shower?'

Warren grinned. 'I shared yours; remember? Yes, I'm OK, but I could do with something for my feet. Did you find anything in here?'

'No, but there's some sleeping-bags in the locker; we could wrap those around us.'

'Good idea. How are you feeling now?'

'Fine.' She gave a tremulous smile. 'I thought I'd never get warm again.'

'We were lucky to find this.'

'Yes.' Miranda knew she had a whole lot of apologising and thanking to do, but the brandy was making her feel very sleepy.

She drank the last drop of coffee and Warren stood up. 'Want another?'

He went along to the galley to make it and Miranda roused herself to get out the sleeping-bags, but found that instead of two as she'd thought, there was only a big double one, so worn that the owners mustn't have thought it worth taking off the boat. She left it in the cabin and went through to the neat galley. A kettle was on the gas hob but Warren wasn't there. For a moment a flash of fear at being alone filled her and she called out, 'Warren!' on a note of alarm.

He came quickly back. 'Yes? What is it?' He spoke with sharp concern.

Relief flooded through her and she flushed at her own stupidity. 'Nothing, really. I . . . There's only one sleeping bag.'

'You must take it, then. Look what I've found.' He held up a half-full bottle of whisky. 'It was in the other cabin.'

'Isn't there any food?'

''Fraid not. Are you hungry?' And, when she nodded, 'You should have eaten some of the Chinese at your sister's place.'

Miranda laughed and he shot her an enquiring look. 'You sound like your old self again,' she told him.

'Bad as that, was I?'

Her eyes shadowed. 'You had every right to be,' she said huskily.

'Forget about that now,' Warren instructed firmly. 'Come on, go back to the cabin where it's warmer.'

He came back with her and lowered the table so that it joined with the seats to form a bed. 'That's clever,' Miranda remarked. 'You must know about boats.'

'A little. You can climb into the sleeping-bag now.' Miranda didn't need any encouragement; it was better but her feet still felt icy cold.

The whistle of the boiling kettle drew Warren to the galley to make the coffee and carry it back. 'I've put our clothes to dry,' he told her. 'Here, we might as well finish off the cognac.' He shared what was left in his hip-flask between the two mugs.

'That's a nice flask,' Miranda remarked. 'Are those your initials on it?'

'Yes. It was a present,' he explained.

From a girlfriend? she wondered, but he didn't enlarge and she didn't like to ask. There was so little that she really knew about him. He might even be engaged to be married or have a live-in partner. He seemed so big and capable, completely able to handle the perilous situation in which they'd found themselves. He sat down beside her on the bed, his legs stretched out in the old jeans. She chuckled and he raised an eyebrow. 'We look like a pair of old tramps,' she explained.

'So we do.' His eyes went over her blonde hair that had gone into curls with the damp, at her face washed clean of make-up. 'Your yuppy boyfriend would hardly recognise you.'

'What makes you think my boyfriend is a yuppy?' Miranda asked curiously.

'Oh, I think that's the type you'd go for—it's certainly the only type who could hope to keep up or compete with you.'

'Going out with someone isn't a competition,' she pointed out, her voice hardening.

'I bet it is with you. Who is your boyfriend? He works with you, doesn't he?'

'How do you know that?'

'I heard you tell your secretary to cancel your date with him for tonight.' He glanced at his watch. 'Or for last night, rather. You and he should make a good pair—a pair of headhunters,' he said derisively.

Miranda found that she didn't like that description. 'He's my boss,' she said defensively.

Warren turned to study her face. 'That figures.'

'Why? Why does it figure?' she demanded, finding that she disliked him analysing her like this.

'Because your type always goes for power; you have no respect for people who are lower or on an equal level to you. You want to climb and you can only look up the ladder, not down or sideways.'

'That is completely untrue,' Miranda said shortly. 'And I am *not* a type!'

Warren laughed. 'That's better. Now *you're* back to normal again, too.'

She stared at him for a moment, then relaxed and leaned back against the wall. 'Is that a built-in radio?' She pointed to a unit on the far wall.

'Could be. Let's try it.' After fiddling with the knobs for a few minutes Warren succeeded in getting a programme of music from old shows. 'Hardly fitting music for a snowstorm, but OK for this time of night, I suppose.'

'What time is it?'

'Almost two-thirty.'

'How are we going to get out of here in the morning?'

He shrugged. 'Don't worry about it now. We'll work something out.'

She was silent for a while, listening to the music, but presently said, 'Can I have some of that whisky?'

'Of course.' He poured a very generous helping into her mug. 'Are you still cold?'

'It's my feet; they just won't get warm.'

'Here, give them to me.'

Her eyes flew up to meet his. 'Oh, but I . . .'

Her voice trailed off as she saw him put aside his mug and hold his hands ready, and she obediently pulled her legs out of the bag and put her feet in his lap. His hands were so warm on her poor feet that she gave a groan of pleasure as he began to gently rub and massage them, first one foot and then the other. They began to tingle as he brought life into them again and Miranda's groan turned into a contented purr.

'Oh, that is absolutely fantastic. Wonderful.'

He went on stroking them, sending delicious sensations over her whole body, and didn't seem in any hurry to stop, but eventually he said, 'Warm enough now? You'd better get back into the sleeping-bag, then.'

She wriggled back inside but stayed sitting up. The whisky in her mug had gone down quite a bit. Miranda wasn't used to it and began to feel light-headed and knew that the drink was starting to get to her. She looked at Warren, leaning against the wall beside her. 'Are your feet cold?'

Warren nodded. 'Mm, a little.'

'Then why don't you . . .? I mean, it's a double sleeping bag and there's plenty of room . . . So why don't you . . .?' She lifted heavy-lidded eyes to meet the astonished amusement in his. 'Oh, darn it! Why be cold out there when we can both be warm in here?'

'Thank you,' Warren said gravely, and slid in beside her.

The bag had seemed quite big but it was surprising how little room there was left when two people were sharing it. They were squeezed quite closely together, their bodies touching all the way down. And his feet were cold.

'More whisky?' Warren asked.

They sat and drank in silence for a while until Miranda became aware that the boat, which had been swaying in the wind, wasn't moving so much now. She remarked on it to Warren. 'And the wind doesn't seem so noisy.'

'Maybe it's easing up. Don't worry, we'll be able to get help tomorrow.'

Turning her head, Miranda gave him a languorous smile. 'I'm not worried,' she said, meaning it. Then, still rankled by their earlier conversation, she said, 'Would you call yourself a yuppy?'

'Certainly not!' Warren laughed.

'Why not?'

'Because I've got where I wanted to go. Opening my company was my big ambition. Now that I've done that, all I want to do is to consolidate it and build it up.'

'It means a lot to you, doesn't it?'

His eyes settled on her face. 'Yes. It does.'

With difficulty she said, 'Have I—have I ruined it for you?'

He shrugged, his shoulder against hers. 'You might have caused a set-back but you certainly won't put me out of business. Now that I know who the people are that you've headhunted I can try and persuade them to stay. It will probably push up the wages bill,' he added wryly, 'but that can't be helped if I want to keep them. And they're a good team; I don't want to break it up.'

'You must hate me,' Miranda said ruefully.

Reaching out, Warren ran the back of his finger down her cheek and round her chin. 'No, I don't hate you. I understand why you did it. If someone had treated my sister so shamefully I'd want to get back at him, too.'

'Would you?' Miranda's eyes searched his face. 'You really mean it?'

'Of course.'

She sighed. 'Good. I don't want you to hate me.'

'No?'

'No.' She nestled against his shoulder as Warren put his arm round her. 'This is nice.'

He laughed. 'What a strange mixture you are.'

'Am I?'

'Mm.' He bent to kiss her nose, then found that Miranda had tilted her head so that he had no trouble in finding her lips.

The dimly lit cabin had become very warm now and Miranda could feel the heat coursing through her body. When she drew away from him her eyes were dark and her voice husky. 'Have you got a sister?'

'No.' He took the empty mug from her and set it aside, then drew her to him and kissed her again.

It was a lot longer before they parted this time and somehow they had slipped down into the sleeping-bag and were lying side by side. Slowly Miranda lifted her hand and began to trace the strong outline of his face. 'You saved my life when I fell in the river; I haven't thanked you for that yet.' And she leaned forward to gently caress his lips with hers.

'Is this gratitude, then?' Warren asked thickly, his eyes on her face.

Miranda shook her head wonderingly. 'No,' she said softly. 'This is warmth, and closeness, and—and . . .'

'And desire?'

'Yes.' She said the word on a note of surprised discovery.

Reaching out, Warren drew the sweat-shirt over her head and put his hand on her breast. 'This is sex, then,' he said huskily.

'Yes,' she breathed. 'This is sex.' And surrendered to the overwhelming need to love and be loved.

CHAPTER FOUR

WARREN had said that he had some experience of women, but Miranda found that to be an understatement; he was a marvellous lover. On the gently swaying boat, in the close confines of the sleeping-bag, he made love to her with an abandoned passion that lifted her to the heights of ecstasy time and again. But Miranda did her share of giving, too, so filled by sensual pleasure that she was overwhelmed by the need to return this joy and excitement, to make Warren groan in gratification as she cried out his name at the climax of passion.

They slept, afterwards, but the light was still on and Miranda stirred an hour or so later, wondering why her bed was so hard, and realising with a gasp that she was held against the length of a man's naked body. Her eyes flew open as she remembered. Warren was still asleep, breathing steadily, his long lashes brushing his cheeks and giving him a vulnerable look that he didn't have when awake. One arm was under her head, acting as a pillow, but the other lay across her, heavy and possessive. She stared at his face, realising that she'd given herself to a man she'd known for less than twenty-four hours; that she'd behaved in a way that she wouldn't have hesitated to condemn as cheap in anyone else. But somehow she didn't feel in the least cheap; she felt as if her whole body had come alive for the first time. She was filled with such inner happiness that her eyes shone with its radiance. She glowed with sexual contentment. Miranda smiled—and deliberately began to move against him.

His eyes didn't open, but after a few moments Warren's hand tightened on her hip. 'Wench,' he murmured and nuzzled her neck, biting her earlobe. He held her closer, his kisses becoming deeper as his hand explored her. Then he swung her on top of him, his legs twined with hers, their bodies moving together as passion flared again and carried them to a frenzy of shared paroxysms of delight.

Slowly they relaxed, hearts thumping, their skin dewy with perspiration. Warren kissed her gently, tenderly, and put her at his side again, his arms around her. Miranda gave a long, unsteady sigh, her body on fire, her breath catching in her throat, knowing that nothing had ever been this good before. 'I'm so hot,' she murmured.

Warren chuckled, a laugh of sheer contentment deep in his throat. 'Lady, you can say that again!' And then she was laughing with him, and knew a moment of that pure happiness that was so seldom felt in a person's lifetime, before she fell asleep again with her head against his chest.

When Miranda woke again it was morning; strips of pale light edged the cabin curtains and the air felt cold outside the cosy warmth of the sleeping bag. Her head felt a little muzzy from all the drink and her throat was dry, but otherwise she felt fine. Warren still had his arms around her but she had her back to him this time. A small smile lit her mouth as she thought how easy it would be to rouse him sexually. For a few moments she considered doing so, but there was plenty of time, and she was enjoying lying here in his arms. So she lay very still as she let her thoughts roam back over the night.

How strange that it should have ended like this; they had started yesterday as mortal enemies, then had come that long ride to find Rosalind and learn that she had made the most terrible mistake. And later the snowstorm and her fall in the river, and then this.

Miranda realised that she ought to be thoroughly ashamed of herself, but found it impossible to feel anything but gratitude for a night of such overwhelming rapture. Had it been the same for Warren? she wondered. He had certainly seemed to be as lost in passion, but for Miranda it had been more than that; it had been a revelation. But she wasn't sure if he had felt the same. When he woke would there be a glow of satisfaction and triumph in his face, would his eyes fill with joy when he saw her in his arms, and would he kiss her and love her all over again? She felt a great surge of longing for him to do so, and this time felt herself blush all over at the force of her own libido.

She wondered what would happen when they got back to London. Warren would have the people she'd headhunted to sort out, of course, but she was completely confident now that he'd be able to do so. How she'd reversed her opinion of him since she'd found out he wasn't Rosalind's ex-lover, she thought with a smile. And would last night have reversed his opinion of her? She realised that she hadn't come out of yesterday at all well. There had been the basic mistake of thinking that he was someone else, of course, but she had also got them lost and fallen in the river. OK, her mind had been on other things but she wasn't normally that stupid. Warren had every right to have a low opinion of her, but maybe last night would have helped to change it. She hoped it had.

The thought made Miranda sigh in apprehension. Behind her Warren moved and she became very still, waiting in heightened anticipation. He tried to turn but found that his arm was trapped, then gave an exclamation and pulled his arm from under her as he sat up. 'Hell, no!' The words were said in a fierce whisper, and Miranda swung round. There was no joy in his face, no desire or even satisfaction. Instead his brows had drawn into a grim frown of anger as he said, 'Damn it all to hell!' and swung himself out of the sleeping-bag without even looking at her, and then out of the cabin.

For a few minutes Miranda lay in frozen inactivity, too stunned to move. Whatever she'd expected it hadn't been that. At the worst, she could have understood if he'd felt some chagrin at their hasty lovemaking, but never this instant and total rejection. Especially as it had been so wonderful for her. Feeling completely degraded, Miranda scrambled around until she found the sweat-shirt and overall, and hastily pulled them on, shivering in the sudden change of temperature.

'Miranda!' Warren rapped on the door. 'You awake?'

'Yes.' She managed to answer unsteadily.

'I'm going to try to get some help. The fuel's all used up so there's no heating, so you might as well stay where you are until I get back.' He waited for her to answer but when she didn't called, 'OK?'

'Yes, OK,' Miranda shouted back, then put her hand in her mouth, biting on it to stop herself from crying. For God's sake, what else did she expect?

To him it had been nothing but a one-night stand—and with a woman he probably loathed. Hadn't he said that she was safe from him, that he wouldn't want her if she was the last woman on earth? It was only the drink and the cold, the need for warmth and comfort that had driven them into each other's arms. No wonder he had been so angry when he had woken up and realised. She supposed that she ought to have been angry, too, because she wasn't into casual sex either.

The boat rocked as Warren got off it and Miranda pulled the curtain back to look out. Her eyes were immediately startled by sunlight coruscating off the whiteness of the snow like a carpet of diamonds. The storm was over, the wind had gone, and it was a beautifully clear, sunny day. Already the snow that clung to the trees had started to melt and drip, making grey pencil-thin holes in the snow below. Warren was striding towards the road, wearing his suit and, although it had lost its crisp smartness, he looked again the assured businessman of yesterday.

If his clothes were dry, then hers must be too. Miranda went in search of them and found them hanging in a drying cabinet next to the galley. They were all dry, even her mohair sweater and her boots, and she quickly changed into them. She would have given a great deal for a black coffee, but had to settle for a drink of cold water, but even that felt good to her parched mouth. How she wished, now, that she hadn't drunk so much last night; but they had needed it to get warm.

Going to the bathroom, Miranda groaned when she looked in the mirror; she looked terrible. She went to find her bag and then remembered that it was at the bottom of the river. Groaning again, she tried to comb the tangles out of her hair with her fingers. Had the owners of this darn boat had to strip it so clean? Couldn't they even have left a comb and a lipstick? She went back to the cabin and tidied it up, washing the glasses and putting them away, then slowly picked up the sleeping-bag and put it round her shoulders. It would have been warmer to have got inside it again, but somehow she couldn't bear to do that, not now, now that the magic was gone.

It was a couple of hours before even the smallest human sound broke the stillness outside, and by that time Miranda had begun to wonder uneasily if Warren had just abandoned her. Then she heard the sound of an engine and rushed to look out. A tractor was going slowly along the distant road— and behind it was the red flash of the Lotus. It stopped and Warren got out and began to walk down to the boat. Hastily Miranda stuffed the sleeping-bag back into the locker and went to meet him.

He swung himself on board and stopped when he saw her. His eyes went quickly to her face, but Miranda had had plenty of time to school her features and she looked at him in icy calm. 'Did the tractor pull the car out of the ditch?'

'Yes. It wasn't damaged.' He reached into his wallet. 'We'd better leave a cheque for the owner to cover the damage to the door.' He went down into the cabin to write it but Miranda didn't follow him, instead jumping off the boat and on to the bank. The snow wasn't very deep and the sun was warm on her face. She began to walk towards the car but then looked back at the boat. Its name was painted in bold letters on the bow; *Chimera*. Very apt, she thought with bitter humiliation. 'A passing fancy'; and that was certainly all it had been to Warren.

She got into the car and Warren soon came to join her. 'I'll get in touch with the local police and tell them that we had to break into the boat,' he remarked. 'They should be able to let the owner know so that he can get the door repaired.' She was silent and Warren glanced at her as he did up his safety strap. 'You OK?'

'Yes, of course.' She managed to keep her voice light, even slightly surprised. 'Just hungry, that's all.'

'So am I. We'll stop at the first place we come to.'

This turned out to be a service station on the motorway. Warren bought himself a large plateful of bacon and eggs, but Miranda asked for just coffee and toast. It was the coffee-pot she reached for first, filling her cup and drinking the hot liquid down thirstily to ease her parched throat. Then she refilled the cup, but drank it more slowly this time.

Warren raised an eyebrow. 'You looked as if you needed that.'

'My throat felt dry.' She hesitated, then said, 'I—I'm not used to drinking neat spirits.'

'No, I suppose not.' He gave her an intent look. 'Miranda, about last night; I——'

'How long do you think it will take us to get to London?' she cut in hurriedly, not wanting to even think about last night any more. 'I have several appointments I'll have to reschedule.'

A withdrawn look came into Warren's eyes. 'Depends on the traffic. Not before mid-afternoon, I should think,' he answered shortly.

She bit into her toast, then spoke quickly, in a hard, brisk voice, to try and hide her embarrassment. 'I'll have to phone the office. I can reverse the charges, of course, but I'm afraid my bag is at the bottom of the river so I don't have any money to pay for my share of breakfast. And if you'll let me know how much you left to cover the repair of the boat, then I'll let you have a cheque to cover that as well as soon as I can get a new cheque book. I——'

'Why do you want to pay for it?' Warren interrupted.

Miranda gave an eloquent shrug. 'Well, it was my fault that we got lost, and if I hadn't fallen in the river we wouldn't have had to break into the boat. So naturally I must pay for it. How much did you leave?'

An impatient gesture of Warren's hand dismissed the subject. 'Don't be silly.'

Her face tightening, Miranda said curtly, 'I insist on paying. If you won't tell me how much you left than I shall just have to——'

Reaching out, Warren caught her hand, startling her into silence. Leaning forward he said. 'Surely we've become too close to argue about something as petty as this.'

Miranda snatched her hand away, her face flaming. 'We are not *close!*' she said vehemently. She became aware that people were giving them curious glances and stood up. 'Excuse me.'

'Do you want some money for the shop?'

Warren reached for his wallet but before he could draw it out, Miranda gave him a blistering look. 'I don't want *anything* from you!' And she turned and marched out of the cafe with as much dignity as she could muster in bedraggled clothes and uncombed hair.

She would have given a great deal to be able to hire a car and just abandon Warren, but without her driving licence and credit cards it was impossible. Miranda began to experience what it must be like to be penniless, or entirely dependent on a man, and found that she didn't much like it. There was a queue at the telephone kiosks and she had to wait until one was free before she could put a call through to the office. She tried to stall by asking for her secretary, but Graham must have told the switchboard girl that he wanted to speak to her, because she was put straight through to his office.

'Oh. Hello, Graham,' she said weakly.

'Where on earth are you? I've been trying to reach you all last night and this morning. I even rang your parents in case you'd gone there.'

'No, I—er—had to go to York to see my sister, and there was a terrible snowstorm so I had to stay the night.'

'A snowstorm? We didn't have one here.'

'Well, you are a few hundred miles further south, Graham,' Miranda pointed out with a trace of acerbity in her tone. 'Anyway, I'm on my way back now, but I'm not sure how long it will take me to get there and I want to go home to change before I come into the office. The only thing is——' she grimaced, knowing how thin it was going to sound '—I lost my door key. I'll need the spare one that you have.'

'Lost your key! How on earth did you do that?'

'It was in my bag, and I lost my bag. I'll tell you all about it when I see you,' she said hurriedly. 'But would you please just send round the key to my next-door neighbour, and I'll pick it up from her?'

'Yes, of course. What time do you think you will get there?'

'About three,' Miranda hazarded.

'You don't have to come into the office today, you know.'

'Thanks, but I want to see you. There's—there's something I have to tell you.'

'I'll make sure the key's waiting for you, then.'

'Thanks, Graham, you're an angel.'

He laughed. 'Anything for a lady in distress—especially when it's you. I think it's the first time you've ever asked me to help you.'

And Miranda hadn't enjoyed doing so this time, although Graham hadn't seemed to mind. He transferred her to Megan, who was as curious to know where she was as Graham had been, but Miranda was able to put her off more easily and gave instructions for rearranging all her appointments for that day.

When she'd finished, Miranda turned away and found that Warren was using one of the other phones. 'I hope you haven't missed any important appointments,' she said stiffly when he joined her.

His manner was brusque. 'No, but I'm as eager to get back to London as you are. I need to have an urgent meeting with several members of my staff,' he said meaningfully.

The rest of their drive was a silent one. Warren concentrated on his driving, but the roads were clear of snow and as they progressed further south all signs of it disappeared from the fields and hedge-rows. It was as if the blizzard that had trapped them had never been, that it had happened in some fairy-tale land of the north, a land that was almost impossible to believe in now that Miranda saw the green fields beneath the trees. She closed her eyes, her head starting to ache, and decided she must think of the experience as just a fantasy, a dream. After today she would never see Warren again, so it would be easy. And she would remember only the wonder of it, pushing the rude awakening out of her mind. In time it would be OK, she assured herself; she would force her mind to remember only what was good.

But remembrance had brought silly tears to her eyes, and Miranda turned her head aside, leaning back on the head-rest.

'Not too far to go now,' Warren remarked. 'Are you all right?'

'Just tired.' And she firmly closed her eyes and shut him out, her headache steadily getting worse.

When they reached the outskirts of London, Warren asked her where she wanted to go and she said stiffly, 'It's OK, you can just drop me somewhere and I'll get a taxi to my flat; I've arranged to pick up a spare key.'

'Where do you live?'

'I've told you, I——'

'Just stop the martyr act, Miranda, and tell me where you live,' Warren commanded forcefully. 'I'm not in the mood for silly feminine games.'

Something snapped and she swung round to glare at him. 'Stop the car and let me out!'

'Don't be stupid, we're miles from——'

'I don't give a damn where we are. Just stop. *Now.*'

But Warren merely gave her a withering glance and drove on. Pushed beyond endurance, Miranda undid her safety strap and reached to open the door. A blast of cold air filled the car and horns hooted angrily as Warren had to cut across the lanes of traffic and pull into the kerb. Miranda went to get out but he grabbed her by the shoulders and dragged her back, then shook her until her teeth rattled.

'You crazy, brainless female! Of all the damn stupid things to do. I'm taking you home, do you hear me?' he yelled as he shook her. 'I'm taking you right to your door so that you can't do any more harm to me, yourself, or anyone else. You are the most infuriating woman I've ever met!' He shook her once more for good measure, then pushed her back in her seat, pulled the door closed, and did up her safety strap. 'Now, where do you live?' he gritted, his voice full of the determination to keep her there no matter what he had to do.

Miranda slumped back in the seat, her head feeling as if it were going to fall off, and no fight left in her. 'Docklands,' she muttered, and lifted her hands up to hold her head.

It seemed no time at all before she was giving him directions, and he pulled up outside her building. She got out of the car quickly, but Warren was there before her and took her arm, leading her grimly to the lifts. She started to say, 'I can manage,' but saw the look on his face and hastily shut up.

Graham had sent the key. Her neighbour gave it to her, looking at Warren in open surprise and asking if Miranda was all right.

'Yes, fine, thanks.' Miranda took the key and went to her door, unlocked it. Then she reluctantly turned to Warren. Their eyes met and for a moment her face filled with pain, as vulnerable as that of a young girl, but then her chin came up and she said as firmly as she could, 'Goodbye. I—I'm sorry for trying to ruin your company. But I never want to see you again.' And she quickly went into the flat and shut the door.

Not giving herself any time to think, Miranda had a quick bath and washed her hair, blow-drying out the unruly curls, then put on one of the rather severe suits that made her feel professional and capable, before calling a taxi to take her to the office. It was gone four when she got there and she didn't go into see Graham straight away, instead dealing with the work on her desk. Most of the staff left at five and when they'd gone Miranda walked along to Graham's office.

She stood in the doorway. 'Hi. Can I come in?'

'Of course.' He put down the pen he was holding and held an arm out towards her. Putting her hand in his, she let him draw her close enough for him to put his arm round her waist. 'So what happened to you?'

'A lot. And I'm afraid you're not going to like it.'

'Oh?' His eyes grew wary, as they always did whenever he felt threatened.

Miranda hesitated for a moment, then said, 'First I have to tell you about Rosalind, and I want you to promise that you'll never tell my parents or let Rosalind know that I've told you.'

'Of course. I can guess what it is; Rosalind's in trouble.'

'She was; she isn't now.'

'But why should that affect me?'

'Because of a mistake I made.' Taking a deep breath, Miranda told him.

'You did *what*?' Graham got to his feet and stared at her in horrified disbelief. 'You poached *seven* people from the same company?'

'It isn't illegal,' Miranda hastened to assure him.

'It's damned unethical. Do you realise that if this gets out our name will be mud in the business world? We could even be ruined!'

Miranda stood, stony-faced, letting him rant out his anger. 'How could you do such a thing—let alone get the wrong man? You had no right to do it. Why didn't you tell me what you planned? Don't you realise what you've done, what you've laid us open to?'

As the second man in twenty-four hours told her what he thought of her, and with equally good cause, Miranda wondered wistfully what it would be like to be a nun. But somehow she thought that no nunnery would be willing to accept a woman who'd slept with someone she'd known for less than a day. Tears pricked at her eyes at the thought, and tiredness let them fall. Graham stopped in midtirade and came over to her. 'Miranda?' he said wonderingly.

'I'm sorry.' She lifted her head and blinked back the tears. 'It's been a long couple of days.'

'Yes, I imagine it has. This isn't like you. You're usually so self-possessed.' Taking her hand he said,

'Tell me the rest. What did Warren Hunter say when you told him?'

'More or less the same as you, really. But he seemed confident that he could persuade the members of his staff to stay with the company.'

'Well, I hope so, but if he does we'll have the companies they were supposed to be joining to placate.' He sighed. 'You'd better give me his address and I'll go round there tomorrow and grovel for forgiveness, I suppose.'

'I'm sorry,' Miranda said stiltedly.

He gave a short laugh. 'Just don't do it again if Rosalind has another broken affair.'

'No, I won't,' she said with a catch in her voice.

Putting his arms round her, Graham drew her to him and kissed her. 'I take it you spent the night at Rosalind's place?'

'Oh—er—yes,' Miranda lied unhappily.

'How about Warren Hunter?'

'He—he went to a hotel.'

'And did he bring you back today?' Graham asked in surprise.

'Yes.'

'Well, I must say that was good of him in the circumstances. So how did you come to lose your bag?'

'It was on the way up yesterday,' Miranda improvised hastily. 'I left it behind when we stopped at a services place on the motorway. I phoned back but someone had taken it.'

'You'd better stop all your credit cards quickly, then.'

'Yes, I've already seen to that.'

They talked some more, and, although Graham was obviously shaken that she could do such a thing, she gradually coaxed him back into a good humour, and found that because she had cried and shown feminine weakness, a ploy she would never have used artificially, it was much easier than she'd feared. By abjectly apologising several times and swearing that it would never happen again, she won him round.

They went out to dinner and she ate ravenously, suddenly starving hungry. She would have liked to just forget everything about the last two days but Graham referred to it several times, which was natural enough as it was constantly on his mind. 'I won't try and make an appointment,' he said, 'I'll go round there in the morning and ask Hunter to see me.'

'You don't have to,' Miranda pointed out. 'It was my mistake and I've already apologised to him.'

'No, I feel that I ought to see him myself.'

'A letter would do,' Miranda said rather desperately.

Graham shook his head stubbornly. 'No, I must smooth this over as much as I can and hope that he won't spread the story around too much.'

'He won't talk about it,' Miranda said with sudden inner assurance. 'He isn't—he isn't like that.'

'Oh?' Graham raised his eyebrows and gave her a keen look. 'You sound very sure.' Miranda didn't answer and after a moment he said, 'What kind of man is this Warren Hunter?'

Not liking the question, Miranda shrugged off-handedly. 'The usual type of self-made man, I suppose. Married to his company.'

'And is that all he's married to?'

Miranda picked up her glass and took a drink. 'According to his record.' Realising that Graham was watching her, she reached out to touch his hand and said with a rueful little smile, 'I suppose I just don't want you to have to face him because of something I did.'

Mollified, Graham turned his hand over to squeeze hers. 'Don't worry; I'll put things right.'

Miranda sighed and pushed her plate away, no longer hungry.

When Graham drove her home, Miranda firmly told him that she was very tired and was going straight to bed, and for once he didn't try to talk her into letting him come in for a goodnight kiss. As soon as she was alone, Miranda got out her file on Warren and rang his home number. He answered almost at once. 'Hunter here.'

'Hello. This is—er—this is——'

'Miranda.' He said her name on a soft note of derisive satisfaction.

'You don't sound surprised.'

'No. I had an idea you might call.'

She paused and sighed; he was altogether too shrewd. 'I told my boss what happened; he's going round to your office to see you tomorrow morning.'

'Your boss also being your boyfriend?'

She hesitated only fractionally. 'Yes.'

'And you told him *everything*?'

The suggestive emphasis he put on the last word filled Miranda with a flash of rage, but all she could do was grit her teeth and say, 'No, not everything.'

'So what lies do you want me to corroborate tomorrow?'

'I told him I spent the night at Rosalind's and you went to a hotel.'

Warren laughed. 'If I ever want to blackmail you——'

'Damn you!' Miranda cursed. 'I wish I'd never...' She stopped, biting her lip. She had been going to say 'never met you', but suddenly realised it wasn't true. She was fiercely glad that she'd known that night.

But Warren wasn't to know that and he said drily, 'You wish we'd never spent the night together.'

'I'd had too much to drink,' Miranda said quickly. 'Otherwise...'

'Of course. We both had,' Warren agreed shortly. 'All right, I'll agree to your story with your boy-friend—if he asks. He may not, of course; he may trust you. But then you wouldn't have phoned if you'd thought that, would you?' He laughed again and Miranda could have killed him. 'Goodnight, Miranda. Pleasant dreams,' he added mockingly.

Graham went round to Compass Consultants the next morning, but Miranda had several appointments and didn't see him until late in the afternoon. 'It's all right,' he told her. 'I managed to smooth things over with Warren Hunter. He's persuaded all but one of the members of his staff to stay on, luckily.'

'Oh? What—what did he say?' Miranda asked tentatively.

Graham laughed. 'I think it would be better if I didn't tell you. You'd accuse him—and me—of chauvinism, if I did.'

Thrusting her clenched hands in the pockets of her skirt, Miranda gave him a tight-lipped smile, realising that any hope she'd ever had of being treated as an equal by Graham had now gone completely. In future he would always treat her as a weak female while he took the dominant role. And all because of one stupid mistake! If Graham had made a mistake he would just have glossed over it and made out it was no big deal, she thought resentfully. He certainly wouldn't have allowed it to change anything, especially his attitude, but she would probably have it thrown in her face forever.

Trying to put the whole episode out of her mind, Miranda plunged back into work and preparations for Christmas. It was a time she always looked forward to keenly because it meant the whole family being together at her parents' home in Norfolk. Rosalind would be coming down from York, of course, and there would be lots of relations and friends who lived in the area dropping in throughout the holiday. Graham was the only child of a widowed mother and usually spent Christmas with her, but his mother was of the 'merry widow' variety and this year had decided to go with some friends on a cruise that covered the whole holiday. 'So I shall be alone for Christmas,' Graham had said when he'd told Miranda some weeks earlier. 'Unless you think your parents could spare you this once?'

'Why don't you come and spend the holiday with us?' Miranda had felt compelled to ask, and Graham agreed so readily that she realised that was what he'd wanted all along. At the time she had felt quite pleased and flattered, seeing it as a major step forward in their relationship, especially as Graham had said, 'It's about time I met your people.' Now, though, she wasn't so sure. Although on the surface they were the same, she knew that their relationship had subtly changed. Probably it was her fault. Perhaps it was guilt, but nothing seemed to be the same since that night with Warren.

They left London on Christmas Eve, driving up to Norfolk in Graham's car, the boot and back seat piled with presents and goodies that her mother had asked Miranda to buy for her in London. The roads were heavy with traffic and the drive took over three hours, but it was a mild day and Miranda enjoyed being a passenger and looking at the scenery for a change. Her father was a farmer and lived in a rambling old farmhouse that had started off being quite small but had been added to so often over the years that it was now a muddle of gables and staircases and passages.

Her parents made Graham very welcome and tried hard not to show that they were sizing him up as possible husband material for Miranda. And Graham was at his most charming, driving round the farm with her father, offering to help her mother before Miranda had a chance, and being kind in a big-brotherly way to Rosalind. On the surface everything was great and Miranda should have felt very happy, but instead she felt restless and, although she tried, she couldn't wholeheartedly join in the celebrations. She felt strangely detached, as if she was outside the rest of the household, looking on.

Boxing Day morning was bright and sunny so she went riding with Rosalind, wearing thick anoraks to keep out the cold breeze that blew off the distant sea, riding hats covering their blonde hair. Rosalind was glowing, chattering about her Christmas presents and the skiing holiday in Austria that she was going on with some college friends the following week. 'Why don't you come with us?'

she urged Miranda. 'We could share a bed in the ski house.'

Miranda laughed. 'It's years since I've done that kind of thing.'

'You're not too old; you're only twenty-five.'

'That's light years older than you—but thanks for the offer.'

'Anyway, I suppose if you go on holiday in the future you'll want to go with Graham,' Rosalind remarked. 'And somehow I can't see him enjoying crowding into a ski house.' She stopped, aware of what she'd said. 'Although he's very nice, of course,' she added hastily.

'Yes, of course.' Miranda gave her a strange look. 'Do you . . .?' She went to ask Rosalind if she had any regrets about the abortion, but realised from Rosalind's happy face that the episode was all over for her and it would be wrong to remind her.

But, as if her thought had been on the same lines, Rosalind said unexpectedly, 'He phoned me, you know; Warren Hunter. Your Warren Hunter, that is.'

Miranda turned to stare at her. 'He did? When?'

'A couple of days after you came up to York.'

'What did he want?'

Rosalind gave a little shrug. 'To apologise and to assure me that he'd keep his mouth shut, that my—my secret was safe with him.'

'That was nice of him,' Miranda said, her voice unsteady.

'Yes, I liked him,' Rosalind said unexpectedly.

Her heart thumping, Miranda asked, 'Was—was that all he said?'

'No, he asked me a couple of questions about Piers. You know, the man . . .'

'Yes.' A pinched look had come into Rosalind's face so, not wanting to spoil the day, Miranda quickly changed the subject.

Their ride over, they were heading towards a neighbouring farm where they, their parents, and Graham, had been invited to an open-house lunch party. But when they rode in sight of it, Miranda reined in and said, 'I don't really feel like more food and drink; I still feel queasy from all I ate yesterday. Give them my apologies, will you, Rosalind?'

'What are you going to do?'

'Ride for a bit longer and then go home. It seems a shame to waste all this sunshine.'

Turning the horse, she cantered to one of her favourite spots, a rise in the ground that in that flat countryside could be called a hill, and where, at the very top, she could see the faint edge of the coastline in the distance. Slipping from the saddle, Miranda went to lean against a tree, the horse grazing contentedly beside her. She tried to picture Graham on the kind of skiing holiday that Rosalind had described and couldn't imagine him enjoying it, either. He would want a decent hotel to come back to after a day on the slopes, and his own bathroom to relax in without anyone banging on the door to tell him to hurry up. And no way would he consent to sharing a single bed, even if it was with her.

But surely that was what work and ambition was all about, wasn't it? To buy space and what luxuries you could afford. There was nothing wrong in that. As long as you didn't lose all the fun in life. Unbidden, her thoughts went back, as they often did, to that night on the boat with Warren. Then, they had shared a sleeping-bag on hard wooden boards and it had been the most wonderful night of her life. Until the morning; until he'd woken up in the cold light of day and realised what had happened.

Miranda sighed and straightened up, pushed a wisp of hair out of her eyes. She knew that Graham was becoming serious about her and after this holiday would probably ask her to marry him. But now, at this moment, she decided that it was all over between them, that they had no future together. Catching the horse, she swung herself up into the saddle and took a last look at the sea, then gave a wry smile; it was just as well that she'd come to that decision—because she was almost certain that she was expecting Warren's child.

CHAPTER FIVE

MIRANDA half expected Graham to propose to her while they were in Norfolk, and gave a sigh of relief when he didn't. But he was full of spirits on the drive back and let fall one or two remarks that let her know that she was definitely included in his future. Perhaps he wouldn't propose, she thought; perhaps he'd just ask her to live with him—or he with her. But no, on second thoughts he was much too traditional to go in for anything other than marriage. And he would never want to live in Docklands.

She gave a small smile and Graham said, 'You look happy. It's been a great holiday, hasn't it? Thank you for inviting me.' And he took his hand off the wheel to pat her knee.

Miranda came to another decision and was about to tell him, but remembered from past experience that it wasn't such a good idea to shock a man while he was driving; she had no wish to end up in a ditch again. So she waited until they reached London and Graham had carried her case up to her flat for her before she turned to him and said, 'Graham, I've something to tell you. I'm sorry, but I've decided to leave the company.'

'What did you say?' He shook his head as if he hadn't heard properly. 'I'm afraid I don't understand.' He gave an uneasy laugh. 'You're joking with me.'

'No, I'm very serious. I want to leave.'

'What's brought this on?'

'It's just that I don't want to work there any more. I—er—I feel that it's time my life took a new direction.'

He stared at her. 'Good lord, you haven't been headhunted yourself, have you?'

'No, of course not.'

'Then why?' An idea occurred to him. 'This isn't something to do with that mess-up over Warren Hunter, is it?'

She gave a small shrug. 'Yes, partly.'

'But that's all over. Look, you mustn't let one mistake get to you. You're good at your job. You're sensitive to personality, and that's vital to bringing off a successful deal.'

'You mean I use essentially feminine intuition,' Miranda said on an ironical note. It was something he'd certainly never said that he appreciated in the past. Before he could answer she went on shortly, 'It's kind of you to say so, Graham, but I've made up my mind. I shall give two months' notice from the first of January.'

'Is there nothing I can say that will make you change your mind? Do you want more money, is that it?'

'No, it is not.' She gave him an angry look at the suggestion.

Coming over to her, he put his hands on her arms. 'You said that the affair with Warren Hunter was only partly why you wanted to leave; does the other part have anything to do with me?'

Miranda's heart had skipped a beat at his choice of words but she realised he didn't mean 'affair' in the romantic sense. She nodded, and her chin came up. 'Yes. I—I think that we're getting too close.'

'*Too* close?' His face hardened. 'I thought we were close already. I thought that was what you wanted.'

'So did I,' Miranda admitted honestly. 'But I'm afraid my feelings have changed. I'm sorry, but I think it was seeing you in my home surroundings that made me realise that—that I don't want to get serious.'

Graham stared at her and dropped his arms. 'I see. And just what was it that I did at your parents' house that convinced you that I was all wrong for you?' he demanded harshly. 'I thought I got on very well with your parents.'

'You did. I think they liked you. It was nothing that you did, or didn't do.' She shook her head helplessly. 'I told you; I'm the one who's changed. I'm sorry, I didn't want to hurt you. I——'

Graham gave a loud, unnatural laugh. 'Oh, I'm not hurt—just bloody annoyed at the time I've wasted on you.' He walked to the door. 'I'll expect you at the office tomorrow morning. Sharp at nine, not when you feel like coming in as you usually do. Goodnight.' And he slammed out of the flat.

When he'd gone Miranda gave a long, shuddering sigh and slowly relaxed. There were marks on her hands where her nails had dug in as she'd clenched her fists. Her head ached from pent-up tension, and she had a feeling that she hadn't handled it very well, but at least it was over now; she'd told Graham and it was finished. He wasn't the kind of man to pursue her and beg her to change her mind; he would take her rejection as a personal insult, which in a way she supposed it was. Miranda sighed again—she hadn't wanted to hurt him but there had been no help for it. The next few weeks at work weren't going to be very pleasant, but she would try to keep out of Graham's way as much as possible, and she had quite a lot of holiday leave due to her which she could use to shorten the time she would have to work.

So now all she had to do was to decide whether she was going to keep this baby or have an abortion. New Year's Eve Miranda spent alone at home instead of going to the big party given by a neighbour of Graham's in Wimbledon, to which they'd been invited. It was the first time she'd ever been by herself on that night in her life, and she couldn't help but feel lonely. At just after midnight she rang her parents to wish them a happy New Year and made out that she was having a wonderful time so that they wouldn't worry about her. There was plenty of time yet to tell them about Graham, when she finally reached a decision about her future.

That decision! It hung over her head like a great black cloud. Leaning back in her chair, Miranda raised her glass in a solitary toast, pushing making a decision aside and wondering what Warren was doing tonight—and who with. He was so experienced; he must have a string of women he went around with, if not one special one. Perhaps that was why he had cursed when he had woken up; perhaps he had wanted to be faithful to the girl in his life. Miranda realised that she would never know; that, whatever she finally decided, Warren wouldn't play any part in her life. There was no way she was ever going to slap a paternity order on to him. The decision must be hers and so must the responsibility, either way.

And neither was she going to saddle her parents with an illegitimate grandchild while she continued her career. Although they would love it, she was sure, and would want to help her all they could, but it wouldn't be fair on them when they had reached the time of life when they could rightly expect to relax and take life easier. Their feelings and happiness also had to be taken into consideration.

January was always a busy time at Executive Search Consultants. Companies who had hung fire over Christmas were calling and asking for new employees to replace those who had left or retired at the end of the year. Miranda was kept busy, especially as Graham pushed a lot of boring research work at her, his look cold and long-suffering. Everyone in the company soon realised that they had broken up, and were both curious and sad when they heard that Miranda was leaving. Miranda didn't allay their curiosity and she was quite sure that Graham wouldn't either; he was far too proud for that.

One day in mid-January Megan rang through to her office and said in a strange kind of voice, 'There's an—er—gentleman here who wants to see you. He's looking for a new sales manager.'

'He's here? But I don't have an appointment with anyone?'

'No, he says that he's talked with Graham, and Graham told him to come along at any time.'

'I see. You'd better bring him in, then,' Miranda answered in some puzzlement. 'What's his name?'

'Mr Hunter of Compass Consultants,' Megan said, and put the phone down.

'Hey! Wait!'

But it was too late; a few seconds later Megan rapped on the door and ushered Warren in, keeping a wary distance from him as she remembered that he had almost knocked her out of the way the last time he'd burst into Miranda's office. But this time he strolled casually in, his thumbs hooked into his trouser pockets, completely at ease.

Miranda, on the other hand, got nervously to her feet. 'What do you want?' she demanded agitatedly.

Warren's eyebrows rose. 'To consult you on a business matter.' His eyes met hers. 'What else?'

'Oh.' Miranda looked quickly down at her desk. 'I really don't see why you want to come here after—well, after...'

'After your monumental mistake, I think you're trying to say,' Warren supplied for her. 'But that's precisely why I'm here. Your boyfriend promised that he would headhunt—I beg your pardon—search for,' he corrected himself with heavy irony, 'a new sales manager to replace the one you stole from me.'

'I see. Well, perhaps it would be best if you saw Graham—Mr Allen, then.'

'I've already spoken to him on the phone, and he directed me to you,' he informed her with a thin smile. Then, impatiently, he said, 'Look, can we sit down or do you keep all your customers standing?'

'Oh, yes, of course.' There was a conversation area in one corner of her office with a comfortable leather settee and a couple of easy chairs, but Miranda gestured to the swivel chair opposite her desk. Warren's smile deepened into irony but he took the chair. Sitting down herself, Miranda looked at him frowningly, trying to still the beating of her heart; it had been a shock to have him walk in like that. For a stupid moment she'd thought that he must have somehow found out about the baby. But that was quite impossible, of course.

'Is something the matter?' Warren asked, watching her.

Quickly she pulled herself together. 'No, of course not. It was just that Graham hadn't mentioned that you were coming.' Probably on purpose to punish her, Miranda realised, and felt a flash of relief that she and Graham were finished. 'You said that you're looking for a new sales manager.'

'Yes. Your boyfriend offered to find me a replacement free of charge.'

'Perhaps you'd tell me what qualifications you require and what package you're offering?'

Warren did so, and Miranda tried very hard to concentrate as she made a note of the details, but at one point Warren put his hand up to his chin and stroked his finger ruminatively across his cheek a couple of times. Miranda remembered the way he'd stroked her body with that hand and her own hand shook so much she couldn't write. As soon as he'd finished she said briskly, 'Very well, I'll pass this on to one of my colleagues to put in hand for you.'

'I don't want one of your colleagues, I want you,' Warren said firmly. Adding mockingly, 'After all, I know how extremely good at your job you are.'

Her cheeks flushing a little, Miranda glanced quickly at his face before saying, 'I'm sorry, but it's better that you have someone else do it, because I'm leaving the company shortly so I won't be able to see it through.'

'Leaving?' Warren's eyes narrowed and he leaned forward. 'But I made Graham Allen swear that he wouldn't fire you.'

'You did?' Her eyes widened as she raised her head to look at him. 'I didn't know that.'

'*Has* he fired you?'

She blinked and looked away, shaking her head. 'No. I resigned.'

'Really?' Warren sat back, steepling his hands together, one leg crossed over the other knee, relaxed again. 'What company are you moving to?'

Miranda picked up a pencil from her desk and fiddled with it agitatedly. 'No one you'd have heard of. Outside London.' She stood up and dropped the pencil on the floor. 'I'll put your request in hand and get back to you with a list of names as soon as possible.' She spoke abruptly, wanting him to go, and walking towards the door.

Swivelling round in his chair, Warren watched her for a moment, then got quickly to his feet and caught her wrist. 'Why are you really leaving? Did you tell Graham what happened between us? Have you broken up because of it? Is that it?'

'No!' She tried to pull her wrist away but he wouldn't let go. 'It—it's nothing to do with you.' She tried to say it firmly but it didn't come out as she'd intended.

Warren looked into her face for a long moment and she managed to return his look, but then her eyes dropped away. But thankfully he must have believed her, because he let her go and stood back. He gave a curt nod. 'All right, let me know as soon as you've found a list of possibles.'

When he'd gone Miranda sat at her desk with her head in her hands, feeling shattered, but she sat up when Megan poked her head round the door.

'Want a coffee?'

Miranda nodded gratefully. 'Please. Black and strong.'

She couldn't settle to any more work that morning, just sat and gazed blankly down at her desk, for the thousandth time trying to work out what to do. She looked round at her office, thinking how proud and pleased she'd been when she'd got this job, how it had been a big step up the career ladder. Up until now she had seen her way in life very clearly; a career that would take her to the top in business so that she would one day be able to start a company of her own. And, somewhere along the way, there would be marriage with a like-minded man, and possibly two six-month leaves to have a couple of babies when the time was right. It had all seemed very simple and clear-cut, but now everything was turned upside down. Although it oughtn't to be. She ought to be able to just go and have an abortion as Rosalind had, then completely forget about it and about Warren as she got on with her life again. Put it all down to a rather unfortunate experience.

But somehow she couldn't do that. Miranda found that she just wasn't that emotionless. She kept wondering what a child of Warren's would look like. Would it have hair that curled at the neck as his did, and his long-lashed grey eyes? I must be getting broody, she thought, angry with herself. I must think clearly; I mustn't let it get to me like this.

On the dot of twelve-thirty, Miranda put on the new black woollen cape that she'd bought to replace her lost coat, and went out to lunch. It was a sharp winter's day, but nowhere near as cold as it had been in Yorkshire. Emerging from the office building, she paused on the step to put on her gloves, then turned, startled, as someone put a hand under her elbow. 'Warren!'

'Hello, Miranda. Let's go for a walk in the park.'

'But I'm just going to lunch. I...' Her voice faded as she looked into his face. 'Why?'

'You didn't really expect me to believe you back there, did you?' He gestured with his head towards the office. 'I want to know the truth.'

Increasing his grip on her arm, he led her purposefully to the kerb, waiting until the lights changed, and then across the street and along for about half a mile until they came to the park. Only then did he let her go.

Frost clung to the branches of the leafless trees still, and squirrels and birds, made tame by years of being fed, came close in the hope of being given some nuts or bread. They walked deeper into the park, until the traffic noise was just a hum in the distance, before Warren stopped and said, 'All right, now tell me the truth.'

'There's nothing to tell,' Miranda lied as confidently as she could. 'I've decided to leave the company, that's all.'

'*Did* you tell Graham?' She shook her head wordlessly, but Warren put his hand under her chin so that she had to look him in the eye. His hand was very warm despite the cold. 'Say it,' he demanded.

Able to speak the truth, she said with relief, 'I didn't tell him.'

'And is your leaving anything to do with me?'

'No.' But this time her eyes flickered away.

Warren laughed. 'You'll never succeed in business, Miranda; you're a rotten liar.' He tucked her hand through his arm and kept hold of it as he turned to walk along again. 'So if you didn't tell him, why are you leaving?'

There was no way that Miranda was going to tell him the truth, but she knew that it would take something pretty convincing if she was going to persuade him otherwise. Her brain racing, she tried the only thing that she thought might do. 'It really wasn't because of you,' she told him. 'At least, not directly. But that—that night . . .' she paused, her cheeks flushing with colour '. . . it made me realise that—that I wasn't in love with Graham.'

He swiftly turned his head towards her. 'Are you saying that you—care about me?'

Miranda was somehow able to make her surprised laugh sound almost believable. 'Good heavens, no! That night on the boat meant as little to me as—as it did to you. It was just that if I'd really loved Graham I would never have let it happen, no matter how drunk I was. Surely you see that?'

'Yes, I suppose so.' He turned away again.

Breathing a small sigh of relief under her breath, Miranda went on, 'I must admit it made me do a lot of thinking. I'm—I'm not into casual sex, especially with virtual strangers. Although the circumstances were—unusual, I suppose.' She added that as a small sop to her own pride, but then went on hurriedly, 'So when I decided that I wasn't in love with Graham and didn't want to marry him, my only course was to tell him and resign from the company.'

'Had he asked you to marry him?'

'No, but he would have done after he spent Christmas at my home.'

Warren gave her a speculative look. 'He went home with you for Christmas? It must have taken some time, then, for you to decide that you weren't in love with him. It didn't happen *overnight*,' he emphasised.

Miranda flushed. 'I wanted to be absolutely sure of my feelings,' she said stiffly. 'I wanted to be sure that—that the mistake I'd made with you didn't push me into making a bigger mistake that I'd regret later.'

'So you look on it as a mistake, do you?'

'Yes, of course. I wasn't in a responsible state. And if you'd been a gentleman it would never have happened,' she added tartly.

'How pompous you sound. Just like your boy-friend—I beg your pardon, ex-boyfriend—sounded when he came round to apologise to me and deny all responsibility for your actions over my employees, while at the same time saying that he would do all he could to put it right.'

Pulling her hand from his arm, Miranda stopped and swung round. 'If you've quite finished——'

'No, I haven't. Where are you going to work?'

'For a company out of town; I told you.'

'Strangely enough, I don't believe that, either. Have you got another job?' Slowly she shook her head. 'I thought not. You haven't even applied for one, have you?'

'No.' Shoving her hands in the pockets of her cape, Miranda turned to walk on, her breath creating little clouds of steam in the frosty air.

'Why not?' Warren caught up with her in two strides.

'I don't know. Perhaps I might go home for a month or so. Maybe my whole career needs to take a new direction; I need to think about it.'

They walked in silence for a few minutes, then Warren said abruptly, 'There's an opening for you in my company, if you want it.'

'What!' Miranda turned to gaze at him in astonishment. 'But you don't even like...' She broke off abruptly, feeling totally confused. 'Look,' she said shortly, 'just because the—the experience with you made me reassess my feelings, it doesn't mean that you're in any way involved with me. I can find my own job, thanks. No one has more contacts than I do, for heaven's sake!' she added on a high-pitched laugh.

She went to walk away from him again, but Warren grabbed her and pulled her back. 'I don't run away from my responsibilities, Miranda.' He looked searchingly down into her face. 'Should I feel responsible for you?'

Desperately Miranda tried to keep all emotion but anger out of her eyes. 'No, you damn well shouldn't!' she snapped back. 'I've already told you once that I never want to see you again, and I meant it. So will you *please* stay out of my life?' And this time she succeeded in shaking him off and walking quickly away.

She dived into the first eating place she came to and ordered soup and a roll, sitting in a corner, her thoughts turned inwards. She felt hungry, but when the soup came found that she couldn't eat it, and only picked at the roll. For the past week she had been sick every morning, and even at lunchtime she sometimes felt queasy. She supposed she ought to go to a doctor to have the pregnancy confirmed, but there didn't seem to be much point when he would only tell her what she already knew. Her thoughts flew back to Warren and the way he had looked at her so intently when he'd asked if he ought to be responsible for her. He couldn't possibly have known. No, but he might well suspect. Their lovemaking on the boat had been completely impulsive—there had been no time for clinical precautions. So it was only natural that Warren must wonder.

So what if she told him? Miranda couldn't help but try and picture what might happen. Would Warren, like Rosalind's boyfriend, pay for her to have an abortion? At a good clinic, of course. He certainly wouldn't want to be landed with a paternity order for the next sixteen years or more because of one indiscretion, she thought bitterly. Maybe that was why he'd questioned her so closely: to make sure that if she was in trouble she had an abortion straight away and didn't get any ideas about keeping the baby. In a man's view, of course, that would be a totally irresponsible attitude. Miranda sighed; as a career-woman maybe it ought to be her view, too. But primitive maternal instinct was at war with modern precepts and she just didn't know what to do. Trying to push it out of her mind, Miranda went back to work.

That afternoon she was about to hand over Warren's request for a new sales manager to a colleague as she'd intended, and was halfway down the corridor with it. But then it occurred to her that the very least she could do to make amends to Warren was to find the very best person for him, so she took it back to her office to handle herself. Luckily the request for sales managers was quite a common one and they had lots of information on their files from previous searches, so it only took about ten days to narrow the field down to the hundred or so companies that might have a suitable candidate. Then Miranda phoned the searcher and asked him to get all the up-to-date information that she needed.

Most of the staff left the office early on Friday afternoons, but Graham was being so pedantic about her hours that Miranda stayed on till five, not wanting to give him any excuse to have a go at her. Whatever decision she came to she was still going to need another job, which meant that she needed a reference from this company. It was quite likely, though, that Graham wouldn't give her a good one anyway. He would use her mistaken vendetta against Warren as the reason, of course, but in reality it would be a way of getting back at her for her rejection of him. He was still smarting over it, and had put it round the office that *he* had ditched her. Miranda didn't much care; she had far more important things on her mind, so made no attempt to deny the rumour. All she wanted was to leave as quickly and as quietly as possible, and she wasn't going to run the risk of antagonising him further.

Picking up the folder for Warren's search, Miranda became involved in it so that it was almost five-thirty and everyone else had gone when Graham came along to her office and walked in without knocking. He asked her several brusque questions about work, which Miranda answered as calmly as she could, then he hesitated before saying, 'Have you found another position yet?'

'No.' She shook her head warily.

He gave a snort of anger. 'I suppose you don't care where you go as long as you get away from me?'

'It isn't like that at all,' she protested.

But he didn't listen, instead saying harshly, 'I should like to know just what it is about me that you've decided isn't good enough for you. Just for the record, of course.'

'It isn't you, Graham, please believe that. I'm the one who's changed.'

'Then why?' he burst out. 'We were happy enough together until Christmas. In fact I'd intended . . .' He broke off, unable to bring himself to be that honest. 'I almost thought we had a future together,' he amended. Angrily he walked round to her side of the desk. 'You've *got* to tell me what went wrong. I have a right to know.'

It was obvious that he had been brooding over it, and maybe he did have a right to know at that, but it would only hurt him more to tell him. 'No, there's nothing. I——'

But she had hesitated a fraction too long and Graham caught hold of her arms and pulled her to her feet. He shook her angrily. 'Tell me. Tell me what went wrong.'

'All right!' Becoming annoyed at his rough treatment, Miranda pushed him away. She glared at him, and was suddenly filled with a glorious rage at his nastiness to her over the last few weeks. 'All right, if you really want to know, then I'll tell you.'

Forgetting the need for a reference, Miranda's temper boiled over, and she found herself telling him things that she'd glossed over in her mind before. 'You became predictable, Graham. I knew what your attitude would be in any situation. I could even guess what your answer to a question would be. I found that I knew how to cajole you out of a bad temper into a good one; I could coax you like a child. There was no surprise, no excitement any more. In other words, Graham, you had become dead boring! And I've since found out how small-minded you are. So, yes, since you ask, I would rather go anywhere than face the possibility of a life of boredom with you.'

He stared at her, too thunderstruck by her outburst to move, then gave a cry and lunged at her, his face ugly with rage. 'Boring, am I? Then see if this is boring.' Grabbing hold of her, he bent Miranda back over the desk as he pressed his mouth against hers, trying to kiss her.

'Let go of me. Don't you dare touch me!'

But it was the wrong thing to say and only enraged Graham further so that he hurt her, bruising her lips as he forced himself upon her.

It was impossible to kick him because the desk was pressing into the tops of her legs and she was off balance. But Miranda tried to fight him off, hitting out at him with her clenched fists, until Graham put his hand in her hair and jerked her head back, making her cry out and tears come into her eyes. With a laugh of triumph he pinned her down on the desk and put his hand on her chest, pawing her. Miranda read the intent in his eyes and screamed, then managed to get one hand free and raked his face with her nails. 'You pig! Get away from me.'

He gave a snarl of fury and raised his arm to hit her.

'I shouldn't do that, if I were you.'

The cold, sharp voice sliced through Graham's anger. He looked up, startled, then, with almost as much surprise, realised what he was doing. He had been trembling with rage, but now he slowly lowered his arm and began to shake in reaction as he stood back.

As soon as she was free, Miranda swung off the desk and turned round. 'Warren!' She ran into his arms where he stood in the doorway and clung to him tightly, desperate for his strength and protection.

'It's all right. You're OK now,' he soothed.

Graham's face was very pale, but he had recovered a little and tried to bluster his way out of it. He gave a forced laugh, ugly in its unnaturalness, and said, 'Afraid I got a bit carried away there. Miranda and I were just indulging in a little horseplay, you know.'

'Really?' Warren's voice was scathing.

'Yes, of course. What else? You—you should have knocked, Hunter.' He saw that Miranda was still clinging to Warren and said nastily, 'I don't know why she's making such a fuss—she usually enjoys it.'

Miranda stiffened, and swung round angrily, but Warren said in a voice of silky menace, 'If you so much as touch her again you'll have me to answer to. Do you understand?'

Graham's eyes widened, then he saw the familiar way that Warren's hand rested on Miranda's waist. 'Yes. I do understand—now,' he said bitterly.

'Good. And the same goes for any nasty little rumours you might feel like spreading about her— or Rosalind.' Warren gazed at him for a minute longer, making sure that his threat had gone home, then said, 'Get out.'

Whatever Graham's feelings on being ordered about in his own company, he didn't voice them. He threw Miranda a look of pure hatred and strode quickly out of the office, slamming the door behind him.

When he'd gone, Warren turned to Miranda, 'Get your things together. All of them. You won't be coming back here.'

'Oh, but...' She turned to look into his eyes, read the determination there, and capitulated. 'All right.'

Finding a couple of plastic shopping bags, Miranda stuffed all her belongings into them, and at the last moment added Warren's search folder. Then she put on her coat and nodded to him. 'I'm ready.'

'Let's go, then.'

He picked up the bags for her and she followed him to the door, but paused to look back. What a way to leave! And she had started this job with such high hopes, had been really happy here, especially when she had started going out with Graham. Now it was all a mess.

'It's only a job,' Warren said behind her.

She turned to look at him, and realised that everything she had said to Graham was true and sooner or later she would have admitted it to herself, so all this would probably have happened anyway. The thought was such a great relief that she straightened her shoulders, flicked her hair off her face, then gave Warren a big grin and said, 'Sure. What's a job?'

His eyes lighting with astonishment, he shook his head and said wonderingly, 'You always smile at the most unexpected moments.'

They walked out of the building and it wasn't until they were in Warren's car and were driving along that it occurred to Miranda to ask, 'Why did you go to the office?'

'I rang to find out who was undertaking the job I'd given you, and was told that you were handling it yourself, after all. So I thought I'd call in and find out why. And how you were progressing with it, of course.'

'It's only been just over a week.' He didn't answer as he concentrated on neatly driving through the gap between a bus and a taxi. 'And why did you come so late? I'm not usually still there at that time.'

'I was going in that direction and went by on the off-chance. Your light was on so I went up.'

Luckily for her, Miranda realised. 'Just in time to save me from a fate worse than death,' she said lightly. Then she remembered that she had indulged in that same fate several times, very eagerly, with the man beside her. He must have remembered, too, because when she stole a look at him Warren was grinning widely. She punched his arm. 'Stop it.'

Laughing openly, he said, 'You do seem to get yourself into some strange situations.'

'Only lately. And one—well, that led from the other.'

Her voice had become serious again and Warren
gave her a quick glance. 'How?'

'I told him the truth,' Miranda said simply. 'Oh,
no, not what you're thinking. I knew that I didn't
love him, but I didn't realise why until it all sort
of burst out tonight. I was bored with him. There
was no novelty any more, and certainly no
excitement. I would have broken with him eventually anyway. But it was my fault; I should have
realised sooner, before he started getting serious. I
wonder why I didn't,' she added musingly.

'Perhaps you tried to convince yourself that he
was what you wanted. It happens. Especially if one
person is keener than the other. And he obviously
was very keen on you.'

'Yes.' She glanced out of the window. 'Where
are we going?'

'Out to dinner. And we're almost there.'

Soon afterwards he pulled into the car park of
a pub overlooking the Thames.

'Have you been here before? They specialise in
seafood.'

It was still early and dinner wasn't being served
yet, but there was a comfortable bar with an open
fire where they sat to wait. It seemed strange being
with Warren socially like this. Although they had
been so intimate, they still hardly knew one another, and the memory of his anger when he had
woken after their night together acted as a
compelling restraint.

He bought drinks for them and sat next to her
on a small settee beside the fire. 'I've always
thought it would be nice to have a house with a
real fire,' he remarked.

'Do you live in London?' she asked stiltedly.

'Yes, I have a flat in Pimlico.'

Miranda would have liked to ask him if he lived there alone, but it was none of her business. Instead she said, 'I really don't know what I'm doing here. I should have asked you to drop me at a tube station.'

Warren studied her face for a moment, then said, 'We really don't know each other very well, do we? Despite——'

'Knowing each other wasn't—necessary,' Miranda said quickly. 'It isn't now.'

Warren's brows flickered. 'Oh, I don't know. It might be interesting to start again. After all, we must have had something going for us.'

Deciding that the conversation was getting much too personal, Miranda said, 'I've never just walked out of a job before. I was supposed to work for another two weeks.'

'You're not going back,' Warren said in a tone that was more like an order.

She glanced at him, wondering why he should care. 'No, I certainly don't want to.' But then she gave a sudden smile. 'But somehow I doubt if I'll ever be able to give Graham's name as a reference.'

Warren grinned back. 'I wonder what he'd put.'

'Probably that although I was useful as a commercial matchmaker I turned out to be a very unsatisfactory girlfriend,' Miranda said only half jokingly.

Warren gave her a speculative look. 'Does it worry you, losing your job?'

'Not in the circumstances, no.'

'You look as if you've been worrying about it—or something. You don't look well, and you're thinner than you were.'

Miranda's heart skipped a dozen beats but she managed to laugh and say, 'Well, thanks for the compliment; I've been trying to lose the weight I put on over Christmas. My mother always thinks that I don't eat enough and fattens me up every time I go home.'

He continued to look at her for a moment but Miranda returned his gaze steadily and he sat back. 'Have you decided what you're going to do?' he asked after a few moments.

She shook her head and reached down to pick up her glass, her hair falling forward to hide her face. 'Not yet, no.'

'My offer of a job is still open.'

She turned with a refusal on her lips, but found herself gazing into his grey eyes and the words died. She wanted to be near him again like this, she realised. She wanted to know him better—and she might even want to keep his child.

CHAPTER SIX

THIS sudden self-knowledge held her still for a long moment, but then Miranda said rather faintly, 'Thanks. I'll—I'll think about it.'

'All right.'

A waiter brought the menus over to them and they were soon ushered to their table in the oak-panelled dining-room.

'This job you're offering,' Miranda said after a while, 'what sort of work is it? Just clerical work, that kind of thing?'

'No, rather more than that. I'm thinking of moving into larger premises and I need someone to go round to agents and ferret out suitable office buildings. Weed out the ones that are impossible and arrange for me to see only those that are the most likely. In other words, to save me as much time as possible.'

'I see. So this would only be a temporary job, then?'

'Yes. I thought it might interest you while you were making up your mind what you wanted to do.'

A very apt description, if only he knew it, Miranda thought. 'And how would you pay me?' she asked practically. 'A retainer, and commission only if I found something suitable?'

Warren looked amused. 'Is that how head-hunters get paid?'

'It's how our clients pay the firm, yes.'

'You can do it that way or I'll pay you a weekly salary, whichever you prefer.'

Tilting her head to one side, she gave him a speculative look. 'Which leaves only one question to ask. Why? Why offer me a job at all?'

'Because I think you'd be good at it.'

'So would a million other people.'

Picking up the bottle of wine, Warren went to pour some into her glass but she quickly put her hand over it. 'I'd rather have mineral water, please.'

He gave her a mocking look. 'Afraid of getting drunk again?'

Sharply she said, 'I'd rather forget about that, if you don't mind.'

His eyebrows rose at her tone. 'You're not ashamed of it, are you?'

'Yes.' But even as she said it Miranda knew it was a lie. 'Aren't you?'

He sat back and didn't answer at once, as if he was carefully considering his reply. Then he said, 'Perhaps it was regrettable in the way it happened, but I see nothing to be ashamed of in two people behaving perfectly naturally.'

'But not with perfect self-control,' she pointed out tartly.

Warren grinned. 'No, there definitely wasn't much of that—on either side, as I remember.'

The way he spoke about it, one would think that he'd enjoyed it. But no, he'd also said that it was regrettable that it had happened at all. Filled with humiliation, Miranda glared at him. 'I've already said that I want to forget it. If you mention it again I won't come and work for you.'

'Does that mean that you've accepted the job?'

'You still haven't told me why you're offering it to me,' she pointed out.

'Because I've a feeling that if we hadn't spent that night together you would still be working for Graham—and you might even be engaged to him by now.'

Miranda shook her head firmly. 'No, seeing him in my home surroundings made me realise that he wasn't right for me.'

'Really? You told me it was realising how—er—easily susceptible you were to me that convinced you that you weren't in love with him.'

'That, too,' Miranda replied, and felt her cheeks flushing. To cover it, she said as firmly as she could, 'I don't know why you're making such a fuss about that night. It was no big deal.'

'So why are you ashamed of it?'

For a moment her eyes grew dark and vulnerable, but she ducked the question by saying briskly, 'OK. I'll take your job. You can pay me two hundred pounds a week as a retainer, plus expenses, and a commission if I find what you want.'

Warren burst out laughing. 'I should have remembered you know how to drive a hard bargain. All right. When will you start?'

'On Monday.' The job shouldn't take her that long, she thought. Only a few weeks. And at the end of that time she must have made up her mind, either way, about the baby, otherwise it would be too late. And in the meantime she would have the opportunity to get to know Warren a little better.

Lifting her head, she found him watching her. 'You look very solemn suddenly,' he remarked.

'Do I? It's been quite a day, one way and another. By the way; this sales manager you want——'

'Ah, yes, I suppose I'll have to look for someone myself now.' But Warren didn't sound all that put out.

'No.' Miranda's eyes danced. 'I brought your file with me. I'll find your sales manager for you as part of the deal.'

'No extra charge?' Warren asked with a grin.

'No. I owe you that.'

'Owing doesn't come into it,' he said, so sharply that she gave him a startled look.

'All right.' Miranda gave a slight shrug. 'Let's say I'll do it to keep my hand in.'

'In case you decide to start up your own head-hunting company?'

That hadn't even occurred to Miranda as a poss-ible alternative, but now she nodded thoughtfully, her brain racing. It would take a London base, of course, but she could work from home to start with. And plenty of contacts, but she had those. Enough capital to get started would be the biggest problem and——

Warren's laughter cut into her thoughts. 'I can see the idea appeals to you. Graham had better watch out or you'll put him out of business.'

Miranda smiled rather wistfully. 'It's a nice idea, but impossible, I'm afraid.'

'Why? Nothing's impossible if you want it badly enough.'

She gave him an odd look. 'That's your philos-ophy, is it?'

'Yes, I suppose it is. If I want something I go for it.'

'And do you always get what you want?' she asked a little stiffly.

'Usually, but there are exceptions, of course.'

Miranda was very tempted to ask him what they were, but there was an amused look in his eyes that warned her not to. Instead she changed the subject, commenting on how good the meal had been.

'I'm glad you enjoyed it.' He glanced at his watch. 'It's still early. Would you like to go on somewhere?'

'Thanks, but no. I think I'd like to go home.'

After the warmth of the pub, the winter air struck very cold. Miranda shivered and put up the collar of her coat. 'It's almost as cold as it was in York that night we...' She broke off abruptly as she realised what she was saying.

Putting a hand on her shoulder, Warren said sardonically, 'For someone who says she wants to forget that night, it seems to be very much on your mind. Now why can that be, I wonder?'

'Because I've never been so cold in my life,' Miranda responded at once. 'There certainly isn't any other reason to make it memorable!' And she tossed off his arm to go and walk to the car.

On the drive back to her flat she became afraid that Warren might want to come in for a nightcap—if not for the whole night! After all, she'd been more than free with her body before; perhaps he expected the same again—especially as he'd offered her a job. That aspect of the offer hadn't occurred to her before, but now Miranda grew silent, ready to fling his offer back in his face if he propositioned her. When they reached her building, Warren stopped the car but didn't turn off the engine.

'Would you like me to see you to your door?'

'No, thanks,' she answered crisply.

'OK. See you on Monday morning,' he said casually.

It was so utterly different from what Miranda had expected that she couldn't conceal her surprised look.

Warren gave her a grin that was heavy with irony. 'There are no strings attached to my offer, Miranda. And I know when I'm likely to have my head bitten off.' Leaning past her, he opened her door. 'Don't forget your things. Goodnight.'

Feeling suddenly very reluctant to do so, Miranda got out of the car. Warren lifted a hand in farewell and immediately drove away, leaving her standing alone on the pavement.

That weekend was one of very mixed feelings for Miranda. She couldn't make up her mind about anything. More than once she was on the point of calling up the clinic to arrange an abortion, the next she was trying to think of some kind of job she could plan round having a child. Several times, too, she made up her mind to phone Warren and tell him she wouldn't take his job after all, telling herself that being so close to him was stupid. But then she convinced herself that she could very easily keep him at a distance, and so changed her mind about that, too. Such indecisiveness both alarmed and angered her; she usually had no hesitation in making up her mind, and once made up always stuck to it. OK, sometimes her decisions had been wrong, but at least she'd *made* them!

This is ridiculous! she thought, and put on her coat to go for a brisk walk by the river. The cold air helped to clear the woolliness out of her head and she realised that she was in danger of letting

the night she had spent with Warren wreck her life.
It had already done material harm to the career that
she had been so carefully building up over the years.
But there was still time to retrieve the situation,
and it wouldn't be difficult to get another job. A
great wave of relief swept through her as Miranda
made up her mind at last. First thing on Monday
she would make an appointment at the clinic, and
then tell Warren that she had changed her mind
about the job. Or, better still, tell him that she'd
been offered a permanent position. That way she
wouldn't have to see him again. And after the
operation she would put this whole thing behind
her and work at giving her life a new dimension.

It was by far the best way; the only decision
really. Miranda resolutely pushed all lingering traces
of guilt aside. This was the twentieth century, for
heaven's sake, and women had the right to choose
what happened to their bodies. And a child had the
right to be born into a stable, loving relationship,
not be the product of one night's need for warmth
and closeness between two people who hardly knew
each other.

Feeling much better now that she'd made the
decision, Miranda turned to go home, but had come
so far that it was easier to take the Docklands Light
Railway for a couple of stops than walk. The
railway was popular with people going to visit the
Naval Museum at Greenwich, just across the river,
and there were several family parties on the train
when Miranda got on. Her eyes were immediately
drawn to one woman, about her own age, who had
a little girl of about four and was also holding a
young baby that she'd taken out of one of the
modern baby-buggies. As Miranda watched, the

woman, her face absorbed, gently played with the
baby, cooing at it and making it laugh, so that it
waved its arms and its little hands caught at her
hair. A look of love filled the woman's face; an
intensely private look of pride and joy, of fierce
possessiveness and lifelong devotion.

That one look completely devastated Miranda;
she could imagine herself holding her own child and
knew that she would feel just as loving towards it.
And what right had she to take the gift of life from
a child, no matter what circumstances it was born
in?

When Miranda got home she was in a black mood
of despair, knowing that whatever decision she
finally came to it would be both right and wrong;
it was definitely a no-win situation.

The next morning Miranda took the Tube to
Warren's office and was immediately impressed
with his present accommodation and the efficiency
of his staff. She felt a passing moment of embarrassment when she saw a couple of the people that
she'd tried to headhunt from him, but she didn't
have to wait long before she was shown into
Warren's office. He greeted her briskly, without any
show of familiarity. 'Morning, Miranda. Want a
coffee while we talk?'

'No, thanks.' She shook her head, afraid of
feeling sick.

'Let's get to work, then. I've written out a list
of the areas where I want you to look and the type
of accommodation I want. Ideally I'd like to stay
on this side of London, and about this far out. But
I think I'm well enough established now to go a
little further from central London if necessary.

Here, read the list and see if you can think of anything else.'

Miranda slipped off her coat and sat in a chair by the window, her legs, in black woollen tights, a short skirt and boots, bent and crossed at the ankle, an unwittingly provocative pose. 'I notice that you've stipulated that you want adequate parking facilities, but space for a car park would add greatly to the cost of a building, especially near central London.'

Warren shrugged. 'I know, but we have to have it. And there has to be space for visitors to park, as well.'

'Do all your employees drive to work?' she enquired.

'No, about fifty per cent, I should think.'

'In that case we could work out the size of car park you need. And it might encourage some of them to travel by public transport if you chose a building near a Tube station.'

'Good idea.' Warren gave her a nod of approval. 'Look, why don't I hand you over to my office manager, Jonathan Carter? He'll know how many people come by car better than I do.'

Miranda gave him a quick look and smiled. 'The real Jonathan Carter?'

He grinned back at her. 'Yes, you'll get to meet the man himself this time.'

For a moment there was a feeling of rapport between them. Warren straightened up from where he'd been half sitting on his desk. His eyes went over her and then he came across and gave her his hand to help her to her feet. They stood close to one another for an instant and Miranda could smell his tangy morning aftershave. It smelt infinitely seductive and she was totally surprised by a wave of desire deep inside her, which was a crazy feeling to have at this time and in this place. She gave a little gasp under her breath and her eyes darkened. Perhaps he felt it, because Warren's hand tightened on hers, but so briefly that she wasn't sure that it had happened before he stepped back and said, 'I'll take you to meet Jonathan.'

Miranda worked hard the next few days. She first did a lot of phoning from home and then, armed with a large-scale map, travelled round to visit dozens of estate agents, looking for likely properties. In between times, she continued to look for a new sales manger for Warren, and towards the end of the week went back to his office to see him.

She had phoned to say she was coming and found him alone in his office, but speaking on the telephone. He gave her a quick glance and waved her towards a chair, but then his eyes came back to her face and he lost concentration for a moment. 'Sorry, could you repeat that?' he asked the person on the line.

He went on talking for several minutes while Miranda went and stood looking out of the full-length window. It had been snowing during the day but snow never lasted long in London, and the only signs of it were the slushy streets and a few patches that clung to roof-tops. Her mind went instantly back to the boat and she wondered how long it would be before she would see snow and not remember that night. Did snow babies feel the cold all their lives? she mused.

Behind her, Warren finished his call, but he didn't speak at once. Then she heard him push his chair back and get up. Slowly she turned to face him, a report on her progress on her lips, but it died when she saw the deep frown in his eyes. 'You don't look well,' he said abruptly. 'You look tired and thin.'

Immediately on the defensive, Miranda said sharply, 'Oh, thanks for the compliment!'

'Have you been overdoing your diet?'

'No!' Then she bit her lip. 'I'm fine. I've brought you the details of four people that I think you might be interested in approaching for your sales vacancy.'

Going to his desk, she opened her briefcase and took out some papers, turned to hand them to him but found that Warren was watching her, his face set. Their eyes met for one searing instant before Miranda looked away, her heart thumping. With difficulty she said, 'Sorry. I'm OK. Really. Thanks for asking. I'm—just not sleeping terribly well, that's all.'

Coming over to her, Warren took the papers but kept his eyes on her face. 'Missing Graham?'

Her eyes showed her surprise; she'd hardly given Graham a thought. 'No, not at all.'

'It must be the wheeling and dealing of commercial matchmaking, then.'

She smiled at the aptness of the simile. 'Not when I've been busy on your behalf. Aren't you going to read the list?'

'Later.' He put the papers aside. 'Will you have dinner with me tonight?'

Her face tightened but apart from that Miranda showed no emotion as she said, 'Thanks, but I already have a date.'

Warren's eyes came quickly up to her face. 'So soon after Graham?' he remarked drily.

'I wasn't engaged to Graham,' Miranda pointed out. 'He wasn't the only man in my life.'

'I see.' Warren continued to look at her intently for a few seconds, then said abruptly, 'Have you made any progress with finding a new building?'

'I've seen a couple of places that might do, but neither of them have all the amenities that you specified, so I won't bother you with them yet.'

'Fair enough. I'll go through your list of candidates tonight and let you know what I think tomorrow.' He spoke dismissively and Miranda turned to go, but when she reached the door, he said, 'Miranda.'

'Yes?' She looked at him expectantly.

Coming over to her, Warren put his hand on her neck under her hair and traced his thumb down her cheek. A quiver ran through her before Miranda managed to control herself again. Looking into her face, he said, 'Won't you tell me what it is that keeps you awake at night?'

Somehow she managed to laugh lightly. 'Yes, all right. The owner of the flat next to mine has let his young brother come to stay there while he's away, and the brother keeps having parties with rock music blaring out so loudly that the walls move to the beat. But luckily he's only there for another couple of days so then I'll be able to sleep.' She summoned up an almost pert smile. 'Why, what did you think—that I'd got a guilty conscience or something?' Putting up her hand, she pulled his down. 'Must rush; I have to get ready. It's a heavy date. Bye.'

Reasonably confident that she'd convinced Warren that there was nothing wrong, Miranda went to the cinema and took in a film. It was important not to let him know that she was pregnant; Warren was the kind of man who would have definite views on the subject and she didn't want him trying to persuade her either way. No, not persuade; he would certainly try to coerce her into doing what he thought was best. But this was something that Miranda had to make up her own mind about. It occurred to her that, if he knew, Warren might feel that he had to ask her to marry him, or at least support her and the child. She shuddered at the thought; they were almost strangers, and, although she was attracted to him and had thought that she wanted to get to know him better, she realised now that it was too late. There was no way they could have an easy, growing relationship with this hanging over their heads. Unless she had an abortion. She could have the operation and then get to know Warren normally; he need never know.

Desperately she tried to stop worrying about it. She had hoped that seeing the film would take her mind off her problem, and it was a good story which ordinarily she would have enjoyed, but her mind kept drifting back, and she was so tired that a couple of times she almost nodded off to sleep. This was silly! Getting to her feet, Miranda left the cinema and took a cab home.

There was a message from Graham on her answerphone; he wanted to know what had happened to Warren's file. He also informed her, in his stiffest voice, that she had a pay cheque to collect. Why can't he send it? she thought crossly, then realised that Graham would insist on handing it over himself so that he could make her grovel. Well, stuff the pay cheque; she wasn't that hard up. Then she sighed; if she went ahead and had the baby she would need every penny she had earned.

Going into the kitchen, Miranda pulled open the fridge door with little enthusiasm; nothing appealed to her except a sardine and peanut butter sandwich. Lord, what a combination! Anyone would think she was preg—— She stopped short, perhaps truly realising for the first time that this wasn't some bad dream, she wasn't going to wake up and find that things were as they had been. Slowly she took out the ingredients and began to make the sandwich. The idea revolted her but she had to have it. The entrance hall buzzer sounded and she flipped it on, saying, 'Yes?' before she'd looked in the monitor to see who it was. Then she froze when she saw it was Warren.

'Hello, there. Mind if I come up?'

Too startled to think of an excuse, Miranda said slowly, 'Er—yes, I suppose so.'

He gave a tight smile at her grudging tone. 'How about pressing the door release, then?'

Belatedly she did so, then went to her front door to open it in readiness for him, her mind chasing itself, trying to think why he'd come.

'Good evening.' He came into the flat and looked about him in interest as she took his overcoat and hung it up.

'Would you like a drink or are you in a hurry?' she asked pointedly.

Warren grinned. 'Thanks, I've plenty of time. A gin and tonic, please.'

She poured the drink for him, but made it a small one, then went into the kitchen to get some ice. Warren followed her and saw the sandwich makings. His eyes widened. 'Is that dinner?'

'My date was cancelled,' Miranda improvised. 'He's—er—stuck in a traffic jam on the motorway. A ten-mile tail-back.'

'Really? I didn't hear anything about it on the traffic news.'

Miranda shot him a look under her lashes. 'You must have been listening to a different programme,' she said shortly. 'Here's your drink.'

'Thank you.' His left eyebrow rose when he saw how small it was. 'Aren't you having one?'

'Of course. Why don't you take a seat in the sitting-room?'

He wandered out obediently and Miranda poured herself a glass of Perrier water and hoped it looked like gin. Suddenly finding the idea of the sandwich abhorrent, she swept it all into the waste disposal and went to join him. She found Warren in the middle of the room, looking round.

'You've done this place up exceedingly well. It's just right for you,' he said approvingly.

Miranda glowed inwardly and smiled as she said a sincere, 'Thank you.' She had taken great pains with the décor of the flat and was rightly proud of it.

'And the view, of course, is magnificent,' he remarked, going to the big, arched, and uncurtained window.

'Yes, that's what made me buy it.'

She waited for him to say why he had come, but Warren didn't seem to be in any hurry, instead asking her how long she'd lived there and how she liked Docklands. Sitting down, he chatted with her easily, trying to draw her out. Miranda answered him warily at first, but he kept to innocuous stuff about her home and family, and her years at university, so that she began to relax, and asked him about himself in return. These were things she would want to know to tell his child, she thought— if she decided to keep it.

The time went quickly, comfortably, and Miranda poured more drinks, making Warren's a normal size this time. His eyes crinkled at the corners but he didn't say anything. 'You haven't eaten your sandwich yet,' he reminded her.

'I didn't fancy it after all.' Kicking off her boots, Miranda tucked her legs under her and leaned back against the settee, giving him a dreamy kind of look.

'What are you thinking?' Warren asked lightly.

'How strange it was, the way we met. That in the normal run of things we probably never would have.'

'No.' Getting up, he came across and sat beside her, put his arm round her shoulders and drew her back against him.

Miranda immediately resisted him, sitting up straight. 'Why did you come here tonight?' she demanded abruptly.

'To return your list of possible candidates for the sales job. Tell you which one I'd decided on.'

'You could have left it in my mailbox,' she pointed out. 'You didn't have to ring the bell— especially when you thought I'd be out.'

He began to toy with her hair, running his fingers gently through it. 'Somehow I didn't believe in that date. Was there one?'

Miranda lowered her head, trying to hide behind her hair, but he lifted it out of the way so that he could see her face. She shook her head but didn't look at him. 'No.'

'So you'd rather lie than go out with me?' But he didn't seem too angry about it.

Her head coming up, Miranda tossed her hair away from him defiantly. 'Yes.'

'Was making love with me so abhorrent to you, then?' Warren asked, his voice hardening a little.

She went to stand up but he caught her arm and held her still. Angrily she turned to him. 'Yes, of course it was. I'm not cheap. I don't sleep around.'

'I know that.'

'How can you know?' she said crossly. 'For all you know I might——'

Lifting a finger, he put it on her lips. 'A man can tell. And I only have to look at you to see how fresh and unspoilt you are.'

Her eyes widened as she gazed into his face. Then Miranda lifted her hand to pull his down, but she didn't let go of it. 'You said you were experienced,' she reminded him, adding with difficulty, 'Does that mean that you have a steady relationship with someone?'

'Is that what you think?' He shook his head. 'Not now, no. I did live with a girl for a while but we agreed to part. I'm completely heart-free,' he told her lightly.

Miranda frowned, wondering why, then, he had been so angry when he'd woken from their night together. She was almost on the point of asking him, but her parted lips were taken by his as Warren bent to kiss her deeply.

She was unable to resist him, not that she tried very hard. From the first moment that he began to kiss her she was filled with an ache of yearning so strong that she was overwhelmed by it. Her arms went round his neck and her mouth parted under his as he explored the softness within. Her response roused him almost instantly to passion and he bore her back against the settee, his mouth leaving hers to rain tiny kisses on her throat and the long column of her neck. Miranda gasped and gave a little moan of frustrated desire, her fingers gripping the material of his jacket.

His mouth found hers again, hungrily, compellingly, while his hand went to the buttons of her blouse and then pushed it aside. Warren lifted his head to look at her, his hand cupping her breast, then bent to kiss nipples that were already sensitive and inflamed. Miranda cried out on a long note of exquisite pleasure. She threw back her head, mouth parted, eyes closed. Her hands went to his head, holding him there, her breath panting and unsteady. Oh, God, she never wanted this to stop. But then Warren lifted his head to stare at her, his eyes dark with scarcely controlled desire. 'Miranda, I——'

Quickly she put her mouth over his. 'Don't talk,' she breathed. 'Please don't talk.'

He slipped off his jacket and tie and between them they undid his shirt and pulled it open. His skin against hers was one of the most sensuous sensations Miranda had ever known. So soft and yet so strong. His hands tightened on her waist and Warren groaned, the way she remembered from the boat. That had been so wonderful, too—until the next morning. She made a little sound of distress and tried to sit up, but Warren drew back and held her face between his hands. 'I want you,' he said thickly. 'This time I want to——'

Miranda stiffened. 'What do you mean; this time?' She pushed his hands away, suddenly angry and afraid, and got to her feet. 'Just because we—it happened once, doesn't mean that you can come here and expect sex on demand. I'm not drunk now, you know!'

'No, you're not.' Warren, too, had got to his feet, a dew of sweat on the broad width of his bare chest. 'You're stone-cold sober—and you want me as much as I want you.' Putting his hands on her shoulders he pulled her roughly against him, moved so that his chest stroked her breasts, lifting her instantly to an agony of desire all over again.

'Don't. Please, don't.'

'Then don't lie. Don't try to pretend that this means nothing to you.'

'I'm not. I . . .' Somehow she pushed him away and put her arms across her chest, covering herself. 'I want you to go,' she said on a raw, unsteady note.

'No, you don't. Why don't you admit the truth? You want me to stay and take you to bed again.' His voice softening, Warren said, 'It was good between us that night, Miranda. It can be again.' He gently kissed her lips. 'It can be even better.'

Swinging away from him, Miranda found her blouse and turned her back on him as she put it on, her fingers trembling so much that she could hardly do up the buttons. Then she turned to face him. 'You said there were no strings attached to your job. Is this the way you keep your word?'

Warren's face hardened. 'No one's forcing you.'

'Then go. Go now.'

'All right, if that's what you want.' He bent to pick up his shirt from the floor.

'Yes, it is,' Miranda said firmly, hoping to convince herself as much as him.

Warren gave her a brooding look as he dressed, then came over and put his hand on her neck, in the gesture she was growing used to. 'Why didn't you say no at the beginning?'

She should have done, she knew, but it had been impossible. Trying to put him off, Miranda shrugged. 'A petting session is nothing. But you went too far.'

A cold look came into Warren's eyes. 'Remind me to ask you where to draw the line next time,' he said sarcastically.

'There won't be any next time.'

He gave her a long look that seemed to go deep into her soul. 'Oh, yes,' he said with certainty, 'I think there will be.'

That night Miranda lay staring up at the moonlit ceiling for a long time, before turning her head into the pillow and crying herself to sleep.

Realising that accepting Warren's job had been a big mistake, she went all out to finish it as soon as possible. She fixed up an interview with the sales manager he had picked out and luckily the man was very interested, so she could safely arrange for Warren to see him and for the two of them to come to an agreement. In the meantime she chased all over the place and finally narrowed the possible new premises down to two sites for Warren to look at. Both of them were within a few miles of his present building, and there was one that seemed to fulfil all his requirements, and which she was quite excited about. Despite all the pressures, she had enjoyed the search, and was toying with the idea of advertising her services in the same capacity. But chasing around had been exhausting when she didn't feel well.

Picking up the phone, Miranda called Warren and told him bout the two sites. 'Someone else has expressed an interest in the one I think you'll like best, so I suggest that you look at it fairly quickly,' she warned him.

'All right, we'll make it tomorrow morning. But it will have to be early; I have to meet a client at ten-thirty. I'll pick you up at eight and we'll look at the first place at eight-thirty and the second an hour later. If I'm interested I can always go back and take another look if I need to.'

Miranda wasn't very happy about meeting him that early but she didn't really have much choice. She tried to console herself by thinking that this was the last time she might ever have to see him, but her feelings were in such turmoil that the thought brought pain as well as relief. The next morning she was waiting on the pavement outside the flats and got into the car the moment Warren pulled into the kerb. It wasn't so cold today and the sun was starting to shine through the dissolving mist. She said good morning quickly, being careful not to look him in the eyes, then, as he drove, to avoid any personal conversation, she immediately began to read aloud the details of the first place they were to visit. But her voice began to falter as he reached a ring road and picked up speed.

'Go on,' he said impatiently. 'How much space does it have in the reception area?'

'About—about...' Miranda's voice died as she started taking deep breaths, fighting back nausea. 'You'll have to stop,' she blurted out. 'Right now!' And she put her hands up to her mouth.

'What?' Warren took one startled glance at her white face and pulled into the entrance to a nearby park. 'There's a public loo over there.'

Miranda pushed open the door and ran, making it just in time. Afterwards she leaned against the wall, feeling dreadful, her insides trembling. It took her several minutes to recover and her hands were still shaking when she went to the basin to wash out her mouth and splash water on her face.

'You all right, love?' A middle-aged woman, wrapped in a bulky coat and headscarf, had come in and was looking at her with understanding sympathy. 'Your 'usband asked me to come in and see if you was all right,' she explained. 'Expecting, are yer?'

Miranda nodded weakly. 'Yes. Yes, I am.'

'Thought so. You can always tell.'

Miranda thanked her and went outside. Warren was walking impatiently up and down by the car. 'Sorry. It's reading when we were going along; it always makes me car-sick.' She reached for the door-handle but found it locked.

Coming up to her, Warren gave her a grim look and put his hand firmly on her arm. 'Let's take a walk.'

'But we have to visit the offices.'

Ignoring her protest, Warren walked along a path through trees, their bare branches outlined against the sun, until they were well away from the road. A couple of people were walking their dogs but apart from that they had the park to themselves. Coming to an abrupt stop, he turned her to face him. 'Why didn't you tell me?' he demanded.

She gave him a wary look. 'Tell you what?'

'That you're pregnant.'

A hunted look came into her face. 'Don't be stupid! Just because I got car-sick——'

'We drove all the way to York and back but you weren't sick then.'

'That was different. I wasn't trying to read——'

'You read the map.' He gave her an impatient shake. 'Stop lying, Miranda. I've suspected this all along. You're pregnant—and the child is mine.'

CHAPTER SEVEN

'No.' THE word came out instinctively, but Miranda meant it as a cry against fate rather than as a denial of his accusation. She tried to break free of his hold but Warren's hands tightened like steel bands round her arms.

'You're not running away from me again,' he told her curtly. 'You're going to stay here until you admit the truth.'

'There's nothing to admit,' she retorted, trying to brazen it out. 'You're entirely mistaken. And if we don't get going we're going to be late for our appointment with——'

'Damn the appointment!' Warren exclaimed harshly. 'This is more important and we're going to sort it out here and now.'

Lifting her head, Miranda stared into his eyes, taken aback by his vehemence. The silly thought came into her head that if it had been Graham in this situation he would have put the appointment first. 'You're wrong.' But her voice wasn't as firm as she tried to make it. 'You're making something out of nothing.'

'And is morning sickness and your thinness nothing? Is your breaking with Graham and leaving his firm not meant to mean anything either? And what about that deeply worried look you have sometimes, when you think no one is watching you? I suppose that's nothing as well.'

She had no idea that he'd been so perceptive, or had been watching her so closely. He knew, and there was no way she was going to convince him otherwise. Sighing deeply, Miranda lowered her head and said, 'Please let go of me,' in a dead kind of voice.

Warren looked at her bent head for a long moment and only slowly released his iron grip, as if he didn't trust her not to turn and run from him. Miranda did turn away, but she reached to put up her coat collar and thrust her gloveless hands into her pockets before she walked across the damp grass to a round pond, its waters grey and still. In the summer it must have been a busy place with its dolphin fountain playing merrily, ducks quacking and children sailing their model boats. But now the fountain was silent and only a few birds braved the weather to drink at the water's edge. Miranda didn't look round but she knew that Warren had followed her.

'Yes,' she said tonelessly. 'You're right. I am pregnant.'

'And it's mine.'

It wasn't a question and she didn't insult him by trying to lie to him again. 'Yes.' She would have liked to look at Warren, to see how he took it, but couldn't bring herself to do so, not after the way he'd turned from her that morning when he'd woken to find her beside him.

'Is that why you quarrelled with Graham?'

She shook her head decisively. 'No. I wasn't sure then.'

'But you broke from him because we'd made love?' She hesitated and he said sharply, 'No more lies, Miranda. I want the truth, all of it.'

But he couldn't have that, she thought, because she wasn't sure of it herself. She gave an angry kind of shrug. 'I don't know. Maybe I'd just got bored with him. Maybe—maybe the fact that I was capable of having sex with—with another man acted as a catalyst. I just don't know. And it hardly matters now.'

'No.' Putting his hand on her arm, Warren turned her round to face him, but his touch was gentle now. 'So we'd better start getting to know each other very quickly.'

Miranda dragged her eyes up to meet his, her own scared and vulnerable. He was regarding her steadily, and she felt that there was even a trace of self-mockery in the way his mouth twisted. 'Why?' she asked warily.

'So that we're not quite such strangers when we get married.'

She caught her breath so sharply that for a moment she felt faint and swayed on her feet.

Putting out his hands to steady her, Warren gave an ironic grin and said, 'Were you so afraid that I wouldn't stand by you? You shouldn't have been; I already told you that I don't run away from my responsibilities.'

So that's what he thought her: a responsibility! Sudden rage filled her and Miranda shook him off. 'How terribly *noble* of you,' she said in bitter sarcasm. 'But don't worry, you're not going to be saddled with me and a child for the rest of your life. In case you hadn't noticed, this is almost the twenty-first century. Whatever decision I make about the future will be *my* decision and has nothing whatever to do with you. You just don't come into it.'

Surprised at first by her outburst, Warren's face hardened and his jaw thrust forward as he returned shortly, 'On the contrary, your condition has everything to do with me. So don't think that you're going to shut me out. And just what decision do you have to make, anyway?'

'None.' Miranda's face was very white but for the bright spots of anger in her cheeks. 'It's already made. I'm going to have an abortion.'

She had never seen anyone look so fiercely angry as Warren did then. His eyes flared with instant rage and he almost snarled the next words at her in contemptuous fury, 'Runs in the family, does it?'

Miranda wasn't even aware that she'd raised her arm to hit him until the sound of her hand's impact on his cheek echoed through the silent morning air.

He caught her hand, his face murderous, then suddenly Warren had pulled her to him and she was sobbing against his shoulder, crying for all the lonely nights of worry and indecision, and because she was a woman caught in an age-old trap.

Warren didn't try to stop her crying, instead holding her close and gently stroking her hair until her sobs quietened and she grew still.

'I'm sorry.' Miranda drew back and accepted the handkerchief he offered her. After drying her eyes, she gave a tremulous smile. 'You must have been a Boy Scout—always prepared.'

'Not always. Which is why we're in this situation. And why I'm involved as much as you are,' he said deliberately.

Drawing away from him, a hunted look in her eyes, Miranda shivered and pulled her coat closer round her. 'I'm cold. Do we have to stay here?'

'We still have a lot to discuss.'

'Not now. *Please*.' She gave him an imploring look.

Warren hesitated, but then nodded. 'All right, but only if you'll make me a solemn promise: that you won't go ahead with an abortion without telling me first.'

Lifting her head, she gazed into his set face. 'Would you accept my word?' she asked curiously.

'Yes. I would.' His voice was quite firm and steady.

Her mouth twisted. 'And would you, in return, give me your solemn promise not to try to dissuade me?' Warren's brows flickered and she laughed harshly. 'I thought not. No, I won't give you any promise. I owe you nothing; you said that yourself.'

'That wasn't what I was talking about, and you know it.'

'Perhaps not. But what happened between us was completely unimportant. Merely a trivial incident, and something that we should both have forgotten by now. A one-night stand,' she said, deliberately being coarse to put it into perspective. 'That's certainly all it was for me. I don't owe you anything and you certainly don't owe me anything— especially something as final as marriage.'

Warren's face had darkened. 'So that's all it was to you?'

'Of course.' Her head came up and she managed a laugh. 'Good grief, you don't think I'm going to let one night of sex with you ruin my whole life, do you?'

'Ruin it?' His eyes narrowed. 'Now I wonder why I feel that you're lying again.'

The sound of voices reached them and Miranda looked round to see a group of children cutting through the park on their way to school. Quickly she turned and began to hurry down the path leading out of the park.

Warren caught her up but didn't say anything until they reached the car. Then he glanced at his watch. 'It's almost nine. We've missed the first appointment but we can make the second.' He unlocked the car and they got in, then his eyes flicked over her face. 'Do you have any make-up with you?'

'What?' She gave him an abstracted look. 'Oh, yes. I suppose I look a mess.'

'You look as if you've been crying—you could never look less than lovely.'

She had been in the process of opening her bag, but Miranda's hands stilled at the unexpectedness of the compliment. But she didn't look at him and paused for only a moment before taking out her make-up purse and trying to put her face to rights.

They didn't speak again until they reached their destination, an office building on a new industrial estate, then Miranda said, 'I'd better phone the other place and tell them we got held up. When can you make another appointment?'

Warren pursed his lips in thought. 'Ask them if six-thirty this evening will be convenient.'

'All right.'

She went off to make the phone call, afterwards joining Warren on his tour round the building. He asked a lot of questions, she noticed, and his whole attention seemed to be given to what he was doing. His emotions appeared to be under complete control, and anyone seeing him would never have imagined that he had just been faced with the news that he was an expectant father. She tried not to wonder what kind of father he would make because she would never know; and she certainly wasn't going to give him an opportunity of finding out, either.

Promising to give the owner a quick decision, they left the building and walked to the car.

'What did you think?' she asked him.

Warren nodded. 'It's got everything I asked for. And the area isn't bad.' He looked around him frowningly.

'But there's something missing.'

He gave her a quick look and nodded. 'Yes. Though I can't put my finger on it.'

'It's too quiet. Too secluded. You'd think that would be an advantage. I did at first. But there aren't any eating places conveniently near, or a pub for a lunchtime drink. And it's a long walk to the shops for anyone who has to buy food and stuff in their lunch-hour. Apart from that, though, it has everything you itemised.'

'Is this the place that someone else is interested in?'

'No. That's the one you'll be looking at tonight. I made your apologies and told them you'd be there at six-thirty.'

'*We'll* be there,' Warren corrected her.

Miranda stiffened. 'You don't need me.'

'I want you there,' he said forcefully.

For a moment she thought of resisting, but it wasn't worth arguing, so she shrugged and said, 'All right. I'll meet you there. Perhaps you could drop me at the Tube station now; I want to go into central London.'

'What for?' His voice was sharp.

Her eyes widened at his tone, but then she realised and bit her lip. 'Not—not that. I have to pick up a lamp I ordered.'

'All right.' He unlocked the car and drove her to the station, but as she went to get out he caught her hand, waited until she looked at him and then held her gaze. 'I'm trusting you, Miranda.'

She nodded in unspeaking acceptance and got out of the car.

It was a day that Miranda wished had never happened. If only she hadn't been sick, then Warren might not have become convinced of the truth and faced her with it. He might have made up his mind about which premises he wanted to buy and that would have been the end of their relationship. He hadn't needed to go out that early, she thought resentfully, and then wondered if he had done it deliberately because he was suspicious and hoped that something like this might happen. Hoped? Somehow that seemed a strange word in the circumstances. *And* his immediate offer of marriage. Weren't men supposed to do everything they could to avoid getting caught in this sort of trap? But Warren had been almost eager to know the truth and had been convinced that the baby was his even before she'd admitted it.

She tried to think straight and work out what was best to do, but it was impossible to come to any decision that wasn't clouded by emotion. Her shopping done, Miranda went home and lay down on her bed, intending to make up her mind once and for all, but almost immediately fell asleep, not waking until it was time to get ready to go and meet Warren again.

Although he didn't say anything while they were being shown over it by the owner, Miranda knew instinctively that Warren liked the building they went round that evening. The size and amenities were roughly the same as the one they'd seen that morning, but there was more brick and wood than glass and plastic, giving the place a warmer, more welcoming atmosphere. Miranda certainly knew which one she'd prefer to work in, and evidently Warren felt the same, for he immediately clinched a deal with the agent, subject to the usual surveyor's inspection.

Outwardly he was quite calm when they were with the owner and agent, but Miranda sensed that inwardly he was pleased and excited at finding what he wanted, and when they were alone he let it show. 'It's exactly what I was looking for,' he exclaimed. 'And it was a stroke of luck that I was able to see it and grab it while the other interested party was still dithering.' He grinned at her. 'Thanks to you. If you hadn't taken the job off my hands I might never have found somewhere so suitable—and certainly not as quickly.'

'It's what you were paying me for,' Miranda pointed out prosaically.

But Warren was on too much of a high to be put down. Putting his arm round her waist, he said, 'Let's go and celebrate. Where is there to eat around here? I know, how about——'

'No, thanks,' Miranda cut in. 'I'm glad you like the place. Goodnight.'

She began to walk away from him but Warren overtook her and stood in front of her. 'Celebrating alone isn't any fun, Miranda.'

'So call up a friend. I'm sure you've got a book full of numbers.'

With a sharp sort of sigh, Warren took her arm and marched her along to the car. 'Get in,' he ordered. And when Miranda looked at him defiantly, he added, 'Don't argue, Miranda, I'm not in the mood.'

He stopped at a Chinese take-away and made her go in with him while they waited for the food, then drove to Docklands and pulled up outside her building. Miranda started to protest but he cut her short. 'We're going to sort this out once and for all. So just shut up and accept it.' And when they got in her flat he didn't act like a guest, instead finding glasses and helping to set the table as if he lived there.

Resentful of such high-handed behaviour, Miranda determined to sulk, but found she was so hungry that she soon forgot. Warren started talking enthusiastically about how he intended to extend his business once he moved into the new building, and Miranda listened in growing fascination at his innovative ideas and the way he'd thought things through. 'I want to get into Europe as much as possible,' he told her. 'There's great scope there, and now that the Eastern countries are open they're going to need help to bring themselves on a level with the West.'

'But they might not be able to afford such sophisticated programming as yours—or your expertise.'

'I'm aware of that, but something could be worked out,' Warren said with certainty. 'It's important that they get started as soon as possible.'

'Would you be willing to subsidise them, then?' Miranda asked curiously.

'As much as I can,' Warren said without hesitation. Then he saw the surprised expression in her eyes, and gave a twisted smile. 'You're right, it's not entirely altruistic; if I help them now, then possibly they'll come to me when they're ready to progress further.'

And possibly they wouldn't, Miranda thought, so it had to be kindness rather than investment for the future. She gave him a musing look, thinking how little she knew him.

'Finished?' She nodded. 'Then let's go and talk.'

'There's nothing to talk about,' she returned defensively.

But Warren ignored her, and, getting up from the table, went over to the settee, evidently expecting her to follow and sit beside him. But Miranda remembered the last time they'd sat together on the settee and instead chose to curl herself up on a chair at a safe distance from him.

She waited for him to speak, determined to squash any suggestion he might make. Warren watched her playing nervously with her handkerchief, constantly knotting and unknotting a corner, then said, 'I'm sorry that we find ourselves in this position, Miranda. It's entirely my fault, of course.'

Lifting her head, she shook it decisively. 'No. It—we're equally to blame.'

'Then don't you think it's right that we should sort out the problem together?' he said, seizing on her answer.

'No!' Angry at falling so easily into his trap, Miranda said, 'It's my life and I'll make my own decision.'

'But you've already made it.' He paused, watching as her cheeks filled with colour. 'And don't tell me again that you're going to have an abortion, Miranda; if you were going to take that course you would have done so as soon as you found out. You may not have admitted it to yourself yet, but you can't bring yourself to destroy it. You're just not that type of person. Can you?' he insisted.

With a jolt she realised that he was right, and shook her head. 'No.'

'So—do you want to keep the baby when it's born?'

She gave him a startled look. 'Of course. What other alternative——?' She realised that he meant adoption and said vehemently, 'If I'm going to have it, then of course I want to keep it. I'm not going through all that for someone else's benefit.'

Warren burst into laughter and Miranda gave a reluctant grin as she realised what she'd said. 'It may not be the best reason in the world for keeping a child, but it will do for a start,' he told her. 'Now, having made up your mind about that, how about deciding to marry me, too?'

'No,' Miranda replied at once, and uncurled her legs to sit tensely on the edge of her chair, her hands gripping the arms.

'Why not? What have you got to lose?'

'My freedom for a start?'

'You'll be losing that anyway when you're tied to a child,' he pointed out.

'I don't know you.'

'So we'll have plenty of time to get to know one another once we're married.'

'And if we find we can't stand each other; what then?'

'Then at least we'll be satisfied that we had a darn good try for the child's sake. And he'll have a father who isn't just a name on a piece of paper.'

Miranda got agitatedly up from the chair. 'No, I refuse to even discuss it. It just wouldn't work. We'd be getting married for all the wrong reasons.'

Pushing himself to his feet, Warren came over to her. 'We made a mistake. We'd be doing our best to put it right. How can that be wrong?'

Miranda lifted her clenched fists and put her arms across her chest, as if guarding herself against him. Lifting deeply distressed eyes to meet his, she said, 'It would. You know it would.' Then, angrily, 'You're not supposed to be like this. You should have run a mile when you found out I was pregnant.'

'I'm sorry not to have come *down* to your expectations,' Warren said with heavy irony.

She shook her head in confusion. 'I didn't mean it like that. Oh, I suppose I ought to be grateful that you want to do the honourable thing; make an—an honest woman of me.' She gave a bitter laugh. 'But it isn't necessary. I don't need you!'

Warren's lips twisted. 'Maybe *you* don't. But maybe our child will. And have you thought that perhaps I might need him—and you? Or don't my feelings come into it?'

Miranda turned startled eyes to stare into his. Perhaps he's ready to settle down, she thought. Perhaps he wants a family now that he's so successful. And to have the child he would be willing to take her as well.

'You could—you could visit us,' she said uncertainly.

'Would that be trying our best?'

Agitatedly Miranda turned away and went to the window, staring out at the lights of a boat making its way down river with the tide. Coming up behind her, Warren put his hands on her shoulders and gently began to massage them. 'We're not incompatible, Miranda. We both know that. That night on the boat was good for us, wasn't it?'

'Was it?' she said bitterly, remembering.

'It was for me. I thought it was for you, too.'

She didn't answer, fighting back tears, and Warren turned her to face him. Cupping her face in his hands, he gently touched his lips against her eyelids. 'Don't cry, Miranda. Everything will be fine, you'll see.' Then he took her mouth, kissing her with deep concentration. Miranda stood passively for a few moments, but then she sighed under his mouth and put her arms round his neck. Only then did Warren lower his arms to draw her to him. Moulding her to his body, they stood silhouetted against the light as he kissed her as a woman should be kissed, with both tenderness and passion.

'It can be good for us again, Miranda,' he murmured against her neck.

A great tremor ran through her and she raised her head to look at him through eyes darkened by desire. 'We don't have to get married,' she pointed out unsteadily. 'We could—we could try living together. That wouldn't be so—so final. If we found that we'd made a mistake we could easily just walk away from it.'

'Too easily. I'd always be afraid that at the first row I'd find you gone. No, if we're going to do this then it has to be a total commitment, Miranda. I don't do things by halves and I don't think you do, either.'

His face was set into stern, indomitable lines. He was so sure of himself. So strong. And he would take good care of her, she knew that. But he didn't love her; and that was something she would have to live with. Although he might come to, in time. Familiarity could breed love as well as contempt. But would it, in their case? If only he hadn't been so obviously chagrined to find that he'd spent the night with her. If that hadn't happened she would have happily accepted his offer in the hope that they would gradually come to love each other. The hope would always be there, something to work for. But as it was she would go into this marriage knowing it was doomed from the start, that Warren had only offered it because it was the right thing to do. Fear filled her heart and she went to turn away from him but Warren held her still. She felt contained by his strength, trapped by his determination. She ought to fight, she knew, but somehow all the fight had gone out of her. Without looking at him, Miranda gave the briefest of nods. 'All right. We'll—we'll try.'

He kissed her on the forehead, but when he bent to kiss her lips Miranda quickly moved away from him. Unsteadily she said, 'Today... All this.' She made an enveloping gesture with her hands. 'It's all been a bit much. Please, would you go now? I'm—I'm very tired.'

Realising from her agitated tone that she'd had enough, Warren nodded. 'OK. Have a good rest and tomorrow night we'll go out and have a double celebration.'

'What? Oh, yes, of course.' She managed to smile at him. 'I'm sorry, all this has happened so quickly.'

'I know. Don't worry; you'll soon get used to the idea.' Warren gave another self-mocking grin. 'Who knows; you may even get to like it.' Taking hold of her shoulders, he pulled her to him to kiss her. 'Goodnight, my sweet. See you tomorrow.'

Away from his overwhelming determination, Miranda had far more than second thoughts. But at least her talk with Warren had cleared her mind on one thing: she was going to keep this baby. On that score there had never really been any question; it was only the fact that an abortion was almost expected of a girl in her situation that had made her dither about it at all.

But marriage to Warren? By the next morning Miranda had made up her mind that she'd been a complete fool to agree and that when he came that evening she would call it off. But during the day a huge basket of spring flowers arrived from him, filling the flat with colour and freshness. And when he arrived that evening he looked so devastating in his evening suit that Miranda lost the initiative, and he'd taken her mouth in a long kiss before she could get out the speech she'd prepared.

'You look beautiful,' he told her, his eyes going appreciatively over the simple blue sheath dress she was wearing.

'Warren, about last night...' Miranda began, trying to retrieve the situation.

'We'll talk about it later. I've booked a table at Stringfellows.'

He hurried her out and there was no time to really talk until they were sitting at a table in the night-club, waiting for their meal. Then Miranda said nervously, 'Thank you for the flowers. They're beautiful.' She scratched at the tablecloth with her fork. 'Warren, about—about what we decided last night. I'm sure that after sleeping on it you must have come to the same conclusion that I have. That—that it's a completely impractical idea and wouldn't work. Of course, I really appreciate you wanting to—to do the honourable thing, but it really isn't necessary and—and——'

'Are you saying that you've changed your mind?' Warren cut in as she sought for words.

Miranda took a deep breath of relief. 'Yes.'

He seemed quite unperturbed. 'Well, that's a great shame, because I've arranged for us to go and visit my parents the weekend after next. I rang them today to tell them of our engagement and they're very much looking forward to meeting you.'

'Your parents!' Miranda stared at him in horror. 'You didn't tell me you had any parents.'

Warren burst out laughing. 'Most people have them, you know.'

'You didn't tell them that I'm...? You didn't tell them about...?'

'No.' He put a reassuring hand over hers. 'I thought we'd leave that till later. And I think that next weekend you'd better take me up to Norfolk to meet your parents, don't you?'

She raised trouble-filled eyes to meet his. 'Warren, I'm not sure that I can go through with this.'

'Yes, you can,' he said firmly. 'Because I'm going to be with you all the way.' Then he grinned at her. 'But tonight we're going to forget everything but the fact that we're out to celebrate our engagement. And as we're engaged——' he reached into his pocket '—I think you'd better wear this.' And he took hold of her left hand to slip a ring on to the third finger. 'Your fingers are so small,' he murmured. 'But I think it will fit.'

It did, perfectly. It was a beautiful ring of two rubies set into an 'S' shape of diamonds. Miranda stared down at it but her vision became blurred and she had to lift her other hand to wipe away sudden tears. 'I'm sorry,' she said huskily. 'I'm not usually as—as weepy as this.'

'I know. Come on, let's dance.'

By trying to think of it as an ordinary date, Miranda managed to enjoy quite a lot of that evening; it was only when she noticed the ring and reality intruded that pleasure disappeared. But she certainly didn't enjoy their visit to her home that weekend. If it had been a real romance, then there would have been no greater pleasure in the world than introducing the man she loved to the people she held most dear. But this was such a sham that she felt herself to be deceiving her parents, which made her feel cheap and unhappy.

But if taking Warren to meet her parents was bad, going to meet his the following weekend was far worse. At her home Warren had been completely at ease and both her parents had liked him immediately, but she was completely on edge and had been terribly ill that morning, which hadn't helped.

'Relax.' Warren tried to reassure her on the way down. 'They'll be crazy about you.'

They would certainly try to be, for his sake, Miranda thought, looking at him. But they were bound to wonder where on earth he'd found such a pitiable creature. Miranda didn't like that description of herself and when they reached his home in Hampshire pride came to her rescue; she got out of the car and tossed back her hair, lifting her chin to defiantly face the day. His parents were kind, welcoming, but Miranda knew full well that she was on trial and it took a great effort to get through the day. When it was over and the house was out of sight at last, she crumpled like a puppet which had had its strings cut. Warren immediately stopped the car and took her in his arms.

'You did wonderfully well, Miranda.' He stroked her hair. 'I was proud of you.'

She gave a long sigh, her head against his shoulder. 'You haven't got any more relations, have you?'

He laughed. 'None to worry about.'

'Good.' She moved away from him. 'I don't want to go through that again in a hurry.'

Now that the ordeal was over, Miranda fell asleep, and was still deeply asleep when they reached Docklands. Undoing his strap, Warren turned to look at her, curled in the seat, a look of innocent vulnerability in the soft shadows of her face. An odd, almost bitter look came into his eyes as he studied her, then Warren bent to kiss her awake.

Miranda woke slowly, murmuring something against his lips, and not knowing where she was, but then she realised that she was being kissed and reached up to put her arms round Warren's neck, returning his kiss with dreamy voluptuousness. It was only when his kiss deepened sharply that Miranda came fully awake and realised where she was. She gave a little laugh, and sat up. 'Have I really been asleep that long? I'm sorry, it must have been a boring drive for you.'

'Not at all,' he said politely.

He walked with her to her door, waited until she'd turned the key, but, instead of saying goodnight as he usually did, Warren put his hand over hers, and waited till she looked at him. 'Would you like me to stay?'

It was the first time that he'd asked, although she'd often expected him to. After all, he was going to marry her; he was entitled to some reward, wasn't he? She bit her lip, then shook her head silently, unable to find a kind way of saying no.

She sensed his withdrawal. 'Goodnight, then. I'm sorry I'm going to be away for the next couple of days but I'll come round on Wednesday evening and we'll finalise our plans for the wedding.'

'Yes. OK. Goodnight.'

Miranda went into the flat, thinking that his last words had almost been a threat, because she was refusing to fall in with his wishes about the wedding. Warren wanted them to be married from her local church in Norfolk, to have a proper white wedding, in fact. But to Miranda, the thought of walking down the aisle in a white dress was completely hypocritical. No matter that countless thousands of girls in her condition had already done so; to her it felt wrong and nothing could change that. The fact that theirs wasn't a love match also had a lot to do with it, but this Miranda didn't voice. She wanted to get married in a register office, here in London, and just let their families know when it was all over.

When Warren came round on Wednesday she was ready to fight for her way, and was more than willing to say that or nothing. But Warren, as he constantly did, took the wind out of her sails by saying that he'd thought it over and was willing to settle for a register office. 'In fact, I've already booked the ceremony for two weeks on Saturday,' he told her.

'You have?' She gave him an indignant look. 'You might have asked me if that was OK first?'

Warren raised a sardonic eyebrow. 'Of course, if you have a more pressing engagement I'll cancel it.'

She laughed, surprising him. 'No, I don't have any prior engagement. Thanks for giving in over the church wedding. I don't think I could have gone through all that dressing-up and having all the relations watching and wondering. Not when—well, you know, when it's such a sham.'

A rueful look came into Warren's eyes, but it was explained when he said, 'I've already phoned our parents and told them the date of the wedding. They'll all be coming down, but I've explained that we want a quiet ceremony with just them present.'

'You had no right to do that,' Miranda burst out. 'They—they'll know! They must have guessed.'

'Yes, I expect so,' Warren answered calmly.

Her voice sinking to a whisper, Miranda said tightly, 'What did they say?'

'That they'd be there. What else?'

Picking up a cushion, Miranda knelt down with her head on the floor and put the cushion over it. 'My dad will kill me,' came the muffled groan.

Warren laughed. 'He's far more likely to take his shotgun to me. And your father told me that he's an extremely good shot.' Lying down beside her on the floor, he lifted up the cushion. 'Is this a private ostrich act or can anyone join in?'

'I wish you hadn't told them.'

'They had to know some time.' Tossing the cushion aside, Warren drew her down beside him, her head pillowed on his arm. 'Don't worry about it. It will all be over in a couple of weeks. I'm only sorry that the move to the new building is going ahead now and we won't be able to get away for a proper honeymoon. I think it would have done you good to get away to the sun for a while. As it is, we'll have to settle just for a weekend away, but I promise I'll take you somewhere extremely exotic just as soon as I can.'

'I'd like that.' Tilting her head, Miranda looked round the room. 'I shall miss this place.'

'Yes, I'm sure you will. But my flat will be much more convenient for us until we can find a house with a garden for the baby.'

The baby, she thought. Everything revolves round that now. I suppose it will for the rest of my life. And because of it I shall be married in two weeks' time. I shall be Mrs Warren Hunter, and Miranda Leigh, career-girl, will be nothing but a lost ghost of the past. I shall be Warren's wife, my child's mother, my parents' daughter, even Rosalind's sister, but where's *me*, where will *I* be?

'What are you thinking?'

She turned to look at Warren, thinking again how good-looking he was. Many women must have loved him in the past, might even have tried to set this trap for him, but she had tried so hard to avoid it. And yet they were to be married, although they wouldn't be lovers, not in the true sense of the word. A sense of desolation filled her. Slowly she said, 'We'll be man and wife. There'll be no you, or me, any more.'

'No.'

Lifting up his hand, Warren stroked the hair from her face, then began to kiss her. Miranda responded willingly enough, and moaned when he undid the buttons of her shirt to explore her breasts, but presently his hand strayed to the zip of her jeans and pulled it down, moved inside. Immediately she stiffened and tried to draw away.

'We won't hurt the baby by making love, Miranda; it's too soon for that.'

Her hands clenched in distress. 'No, I know, but... Couldn't we...? We—we'll be married in two weeks' time.'

A grim note crept into Warren's voice. 'And you want to wait till then; is that what you're trying to say?'

She gave him an imploring look. 'Yes. *Please.*'

Warren hesitated, wondering whether to force the issue, but then sighed. 'All right, Miranda, if that's what you want. We'll wait till we're married.' He gave a sudden harsh laugh. 'But in the circumstances I can hardly believe it!'

CHAPTER EIGHT

IT WAS a fine day for the wedding, although Miranda hardly noticed the weather. She was a bag of nerves, her eyes dark-shadowed by lack of sleep. Her parents had travelled down the day before and she had spent the evening with them at their hotel. It hadn't been pleasant; her father—a plain-speaker at the best of times—had been downright angry, and her mother upset. 'You could at least have had a proper wedding instead of this hole-and-corner affair,' her mother said more than once.

In the end Miranda had silenced them by rounding on them and blurting out, 'You should be pleased I'm getting married at all. I didn't want to; it wasn't my idea.'

As she got ready, Miranda wondered whether Warren had been getting the same kind of stick from his parents, but decided he was man enough to handle it. She dressed carefully in the outfit that she'd taken a long time to choose. Not because there wasn't an ocean of choice in London, but because she hadn't been able to make up her mind what would be right. She didn't feel like a bride so didn't want anything full and pretty, and definitely nothing in white, so in the end had settled for a rather severe, long-jacketed suit in blue, but couldn't resist a dream of a hat that exactly matched it, and which looked very sophisticated when worn with her hair up.

The wedding was grim, with both sets of parents meeting each other for the first time and trying to pretend that it was a happy occasion. Rosalind was there, too, having insisted on travelling down from York, and she flushed deeply when she saw Miranda arrive at the register office. Immediately guessing her thoughts, Miranda went over to her and took her hand. 'You shouldn't have come,' she said quietly. 'I didn't want you to be upset.'

'Why didn't you—do what I did?' Rosalind whispered back.

Miranda gave a small smile and touched her sister's cheek. 'I'm not as strong as you.'

Rosalind stared at her, would have said something else, but Miranda squeezed her hand and moved away to greet Warren's parents.

Afterwards Miranda couldn't recall a word she'd said or any of the vows they'd made at the ceremony. She stood beside Warren, who seemed more than ever a stranger in his immaculate dark suit, and repeated what she was told to say. But halfway through she glanced at all the long, solemn faces of the watching relations and her voice faltered. Lord, they might have been at a funeral rather than a wedding. Suddenly she was filled with a fit of the giggles and had to put a hand up to her mouth to cover them. Warren looked at her in concern, then saw the flash of laughter in her eyes. His own widened in surprise, but then he gave her an answering grin and his hand tightened on hers so that for a few blessed minutes she forgot everyone else and thought only of him.

The ceremony over, they posed for a few photographs before driving to a nearby restaurant for lunch. Everyone was very polite to each other and the parents did their best, but Warren's father was an architect and hers a farmer, so they had little in common. And the mothers were patently blaming each other's offspring for the situation and trying not to show it.

'You haven't even got a wedding-cake,' Miranda's mother said to her in a grieved undertone.

'Haven't we? I don't expect Warren's imagination ran to a cake.'

'Warren's? Didn't you order this meal, then?'

'No. He did it all: the meal, the ceremony, the flowers.' And she reached out a finger to gently touch one of the pale yellow roses in the bouquet he had given her.

Her mother gave her an odd look. 'Miranda, are you sure you're doing the right thing?'

Miranda laughed, but there was a jarring note to it that made everyone look at her. She flushed and said, 'Of course,' trying to sound convincing.

Shortly afterwards everyone drank a toast to them and Warren stood up to make a brief speech in reply, referring to her more than once as his wife, which felt very odd. It came as a great relief when he said it was time for them to leave.

Outside the restaurant Rosalind showered confetti over them, which was such a surprise that tears came into Miranda's eyes. The sisters hugged tightly and Miranda pushed her flowers into Rosalind's hands. 'Here, look after this for me.' Then she was saying goodbye to everyone else and Warren was helping her into the Lotus.

It was too low for a hat; Miranda had to duck down while she waved goodbye and then took a couple of minutes taking off the hat and re-pinning her hair, which gave her a little time in which to face up to being married and on the way to her honeymoon. As they could only get away for a weekend, their destination was less than a couple of hours' drive away, to a country hotel in Shropshire. Warren had asked her where she would like to go, but Miranda had left it to him, as she had left all the arrangements for the wedding.

'You OK?' he asked now. Adding with a grin, 'Not feeling car-sick?'

She smiled briefly in return. 'No, I'm fine.' Then sighed. 'I'm glad it's over. I expect they are, too.'

'Don't worry, they'll soon get used to the idea. My mother has been longing for a grandchild for years.' He glanced at her. 'Why don't you take a nap?'

Leaning back against the head-rest, Miranda closed her eyes but she didn't sleep. The wedding might be over but tonight was going to be an even bigger ordeal, because she'd run out of excuses. Tonight, when Warren took her to bed, he would insist on making love. Well, that was OK, wasn't it? It had been good between them before and he would make it so again. But last time had been so different, Miranda thought wistfully. Then they had been drawn together by a mutual need, fuelled by a sensual awareness that had overcome them both. Plus the booze, of course, she thought with an inner stab of bitter irony. But this time, what would it be? Sex on Warren's part, of course, because she knew that he wanted her, and her putting him off had only increased his need. And on hers? Duty? Keeping her part of the bargain?

Miranda's hands tightened in her lap and she bit her lip hard, knowing it would be neither of those things. For her it would be as it had been before but increased a hundredfold, for there would be love there, too. Because somewhere along the line she had fallen head over heels in love with Warren, but hadn't realised it until it was too late to draw back, until there was no way she could have drawn back. And that was why she was so reluctant and afraid to go to bed with him: because she knew he didn't love her and she couldn't bear to see him turn away from her again.

When they reached the hotel they were given tea in a room with a big inglenook fire, before going for a walk round the grounds. It was the beginning of March and there was a carpet of snowdrops on the slope leading down to a narrow river, and they had to be careful where they trod to avoid the fat-budded daffodils. They walked hand in hand, and, by pretending that they were really in love, Miranda knew a period of pure contentment. If only it could always be like this; if only it were true. When it grew dusk they walked back to the hotel and went up to their room, taking it in turns to use the bathroom to change as if this were a real wedding-night, and she an innocent virgin.

Miranda kept her hair up for dinner, wearing a deep red velvet dress with a square neck and long sleeves, and a wide black belt at her still-narrow waist. Dinner was an excellent meal but Miranda didn't eat much and Warren only allowed her one glass of wine, for fear of harming the baby. Afterwards they sat in the lounge with the other guests to drink their coffee, but it wasn't long before Warren reached out to take her hand. Glancing up, she saw the dark, undisguised flare of need in his eyes and gave a small gasp. He stood up, his eyes still on hers, and Miranda got slowly to her feet.

Drawing her out of the room, he put his arm round her waist and held her close to his side as they went up the stairs.

There was a lamp already burning in the room. By its light Warren reached up to take the pins from her hair and let it cascade over his hands. Then, his hands still in her hair, he began to rain tiny kisses on her face, exploring each feature with his lips as if he had never touched her before, as if she was very fragile and precious. Then his hands went to her clothes, removing them slowly, one by one, kissing her soft white skin as the removal of each garment revealed it to his eyes. Miranda stood very still, her eyes closed, letting him do what he wanted. As his touch and his kisses became more intimate, her breathing quickened, until at last there was nothing left to take off.

Slowly, then, she opened her eyes to find him watching her, his face dark with naked desire. He seemed to be waiting and for a moment she didn't understand, but then she lifted her hands and began to undo his tie.

The sheets of the bed struck chill to her hot body, reminding Miranda of their night in the snow. But the room smelt of the flowers that Warren had filled it with, whereas the *Chimera* had smelt of damp and diesel. He laid her in the bed, then lay down beside her, the lamp still on, the covers drawn back. 'You're so beautiful, Miranda,' he murmured thickly. 'So lovely.' His hand went over her, warm, caressing, making her gasp and move sensuously. He kissed her again in growing, urgent passion and she could sense the anticipation in him as he moved over her.

Immediately Miranda grew tense, rigid. Desperately she tried to relax, telling herself that it would be all right, *all right*. But then she felt his hand on her thigh and suddenly she had pushed Warren aside and jackknifed out of bed. 'I can't! I just can't!' She ran to the end of the room and cowered in a corner, shaking convulsively.

For a moment there was a shattering silence in the room, then Warren leapt across to her and jerked her out of the corner. '*What the hell are you playing at?*'

'I'm sorry, but I can't. Not in cold blood.'

'Not in... What's that supposed to mean, for God's sake?'

Miranda tried to pull away, to cover herself, but he had hold of her wrists in a vicelike grip. Desperately she tried to control her voice, but could only manage, 'Last time. We—we'd had a lot to drink. So—so...'

Warren stared down at her in incredulous comprehension. 'You can only make love when you're drunk! Is that what you're saying?'

'No. Yes. *I don't know!* I only know that I can't now,' Miranda returned in deep distress. 'Let me go, Warren, please.'

But he was too angry to listen. 'I've been as patient with you as I damn well know how. And for what? To be told you can't make love unless you're drunk. Or is it only *me* that you can't go to bed with unless you're sozzled out of your mind?'

Shaking her head as if it hurt, she said, 'You don't understand; I want to go to bed with you, but I—I just can't. I'm sorry.'

'You're right, I don't damn well understand. Were you like this with Graham?'

'I never went to bed with Graham,' Miranda flared in sudden anger.

Warren stared grimly into her face. 'After to-night I have no trouble in believing that.' Slowly he relaxed his grip and turned away. Picking up their robes he threw her one and put on his own. 'So where the hell does that leave us?'

Putting on the robe, Miranda pulled the belt tightly round her waist. 'I don't know. I'm sorry. I'm so terribly sorry.'

His voice curt, Warren said, 'Well, you'd better make up your mind, Miranda, and fast, because you're my wife and that's what you're going to be—in every sense of the word!'

They cut short the weekend and went back to London the next morning. When they reached Warren's flat he just dumped the cases and went to work, not coming home till late. The same went for the next few days. The company was moving into the new premises so he had every reason to work hard and to just fall into bed when he came home, tired out. From the first night Miranda had slept in the spare-room, but she knew it couldn't last. Warren wasn't the kind of man who would let this go on indefinitely. And she didn't want it herself. She *wanted* to be properly married, to be a wife to him, not have this terrible tension between them.

Instinct told her that the coming weekend would decide the matter, and Miranda made up her mind that she must either instigate their lovemaking, or at least meet him halfway, so that he didn't have to force the issue.

On Saturday Warren went in to work but said that he would be home in time for dinner. That was all he said but there was a great deal of determination implicit in his tone. But halfway through the afternoon he rang to say that there was a problem and he would be late after all. Miranda had been trying to gear herself up to face him all day, and felt an immediate snapping of tension when he said he would be late. At seven she went to make herself a meal but found that she suddenly disliked everything in the house. A craving for something hot and spicy filled her, a craving so strong that she put on her coat and walked half a mile or so to an Indian tandoori restaurant where she ordered the hottest curry on the menu. Bearing in mind her resolution to meet Warren halfway, Miranda decided it wouldn't do any harm to try and relax by having a couple of drinks with the meal so ordered half a bottle of wine as well.

The air struck very cold when she came out of the restaurant. It had rained earlier but now there was a frost and the ground was slippery if you weren't careful. Miranda had eaten so much that the waistband of her skirt felt tight—or perhaps that was just the first sign of the baby growing. Her problem with Warren had filled her mind so much that she hadn't given much thought to the baby; hadn't bought anything for it or even chosen a name. But there would be plenty of time for that; right now she had to go home and face a husband who was about to demand his conjugal rights. The archaic term caught at her sense of the ridiculous and made her laugh. Suddenly it didn't seem such a terrible ordeal any more. OK, maybe Warren didn't love her, but he'd married her, hadn't he? And he wanted her. What more could she ask for?

He would be home soon; might even be there now, wondering where she was.

Filled with an overwhelming need to be with him, to be close to him, Miranda began to hurry eagerly home. There were a couple of steps leading down from a high kerb. Miranda's booted heel slipped on a patch of ice and she tumbled down the steps. For a few moments she lay on the ground, startled and winded, but was already getting up when a couple of people hurried over to help her. Having assured them that she was all right, Miranda hurried on her way again, but taking more care where she put her feet this time. She was almost in sight of her own street when the first pain ripped through her stomach. She gave a cry and stood still, holding herself, then tried to go on, to get home. But the second pain was even worse than the first and made her catch hold of a lamppost to hold herself up. She was near the Tube station and there were people about. Two women came up to her, asked her if she was all right. Miranda turned an agonised face towards them. 'My baby! Please help me.'

There had been an accident somewhere and the ambulance was delayed. By the time it came Miranda knew that it was too late. They took her to a hospital and did their best for her, and were kind when they told her she'd lost the baby. 'The fall,' the doctor told her. 'And too much spicy food on an empty stomach.' So it was her fault, her fault.

'Is there anyone we can ring for you?' a nurse asked when the doctor had gone.

'My—my husband.' And she gave the number.

'Of course. We'll call him right away so that he can come and be with you.'

'No! Please—just tell him, but say that there's no need to come. Say I'm asleep or something.'

The nurse gave her an odd look. 'Are you sure?'

Miranda nodded wearily, her hair clinging to her pain-damp face. 'Yes. I'll—I'll see him tomorrow.'

'Perhaps that's best. I'll give you something to make you sleep.'

She took the sleeping-pills gratefully, and when Warren heard and came to see her anyway she was indeed asleep and unaware that he took her hand and sat by her bed for a long while before going home again.

But the pills weren't very strong and Miranda woke early and lay looking up at the ceiling, not wanting to face the day. As soon as the ward began to stir, she got up and went into the bathroom to dress. All right, so the baby was gone, she kept telling herself. Well, she'd never really wanted it in the first place, so maybe she deserved to lose it. Only losing the baby meant losing Warren, too, and that she didn't think she could bear.

'I'm feeling fine now so I'm going home,' she told the ward sister who'd just come on duty.

Having been a nurse too long to be surprised by anything, the woman merely nodded. 'All right, but you'll have to sign this form.'

A form for everything, Miranda thought cynically; and did they have a form to cover her lost baby? Going outside she hailed a taxi, but instead of directing it to Warren's flat in Pimlico, she gave the Docklands address.

The flat hadn't yet been sold and most of her things were still there; they had been going to put them into storage until they could find a house, but there hadn't been time before their rushed wedding.

Dropping a cushion on the floor by the big window, Miranda sat in her favourite place, where she could see the shipping on the Thames. The sense of timelessness that the river gave her had always been a great comfort in times of stress, but now there was no comfort to be found. She had destroyed her baby, however inadvertently, just as surely as if she had had an abortion. Somehow she would have to learn to live with that. And somehow she was going to have to find the strength to let Warren go; to make a clean break so that at least he wouldn't hate her so much. Although she was sure he would never forgive her about the baby. He might come to look back on this marriage as just a past nightmare, but he would never forget the child. And nor would she. Miranda stared unseeingly out at the river, her heart full of grief and despair.

A key turned in the lock and Warren came through into the sitting-room. His face was very grim and he looked terribly tired, as if he hadn't slept all night. 'I thought I'd find you here.' He came over and stood looking down at her, his hands thrust into his pockets.

'I didn't do it on purpose. I really didn't,' Miranda said wretchedly, then looked away, unable to bear the condemnation in his eyes.

'Maybe you didn't,' Warren said heavily after a moment. 'Not consciously, anyway. But subconsciously I think you were fighting against it—and our marriage.' He gave a harsh laugh. 'Only that you were fighting openly, of course.'

Miranda opened her mouth to tell him that she had been hurrying home to him, that she had really been going to try, but realised that there was no point now, and he wouldn't believe her anyway. Her hands tightened into nail-hurting fists and she could only say, 'I'm sorry.'

'You're sorry!' Warren was suddenly angry. 'Is that all you can find to say?' Swinging round, he suddenly crashed his fist violently against the wall, then stood there for a moment, his eyes closed as he fought to control his pain and grief.

Miranda wanted to get up, go to him, put her arms around him and give what comfort she could, whatever he cared to take. But the knowledge that it was all her fault, and that he would rightly spurn her with bitter contempt, held her back. So she stayed where she was, her face drained of colour, and waited until he'd recovered sufficiently to turn and say coldly, 'So what of us now?'

Taking a deep breath, Miranda said, 'I suppose we'll go back to where we were——' she looked up to find Warren's eyes fixed on her intently '—before we met.' His eyes flickered and he looked away. Her voice raw with pain, Miranda went on, 'It shouldn't be difficult to have the marriage quashed in the circumstances. Then you'll be free again.'

'As you'll be.'

'Yes.' The word was said on a long sigh of unhappiness.

'What will you do?'

'What?' She tried to smile and shrug. 'Oh, I'll be fine. I'll get a job, soon be back in the swing of things.'

Warren stood looking down at her, his face unreadable. 'Are you sure this is what you want?'

'Yes, of course.' But the smile slipped woefully. 'You—we only got married because of the baby; now it's—it's gone, there's nothing to keep us together.'

'No.' Taking the key to the flat from his pocket he dropped it on the floor beside her. 'You'll want this back.' He turned away, walked over to the door, hesitated. 'We may never see each other again, then.'

'No.' Miranda's eyes were fixed on him hungrily, the word little more than a breath.

Warren's mouth twisted. 'So this is goodbye.' He seemed about to say something, while Miranda waited breathlessly, but then he shrugged. 'So long, Miranda.' And went out of the door. A moment later the front door slammed and she knew that he was gone forever.

For a few minutes she couldn't take it in, just sat staring at where he'd stood, but then a great cry of loss burst from her lungs and Miranda dropped to the floor and curled herself into a ball, weeping agonisingly.

'Miranda.'

It took a while for his voice to penetrate, but when it did Miranda stopped crying abruptly. Warren had come back and was standing by the doorway. All her previous resolution and strength lost under the tide of grief, Miranda got up and ran to him like an arrow from a bow. Throwing herself into his arms, she sobbed, 'Please don't leave me! Oh, please don't leave. I love you so much! I know you don't love me, but I'll try so hard to make you happy. And we can have another baby and you'll love that, and—— '

'Hey! Hey.' Warren put his hand in her hair and held her a little away from him. 'What did you say?'

'I—I love you,' Miranda answered simply. 'I don't want you to go.'

Lifting his finger, Warren wiped a tear from her cheek. 'When did you find that out?'

'I don't know. Weeks ago, I think.'

'Why didn't you tell me before?'

She shook her head and looked away. 'I didn't want to—embarrass you. I know you don't love me. That's why I tried so hard to be strong and let you go, just now. But you came back.' She lifted eyes full of hope and fear to meet his. 'Why did you come back?'

'What's all this about knowing I don't love you?' Warren countered.

She was silent for a long moment and her voice full of pain when Miranda finally answered, 'I've always known. That night on the boat; when you woke up in the morning you thought I was asleep, but I wasn't. I saw and heard you. You said, "Hell, no!" and you turned away with such a look of anger and dismay on your face that I knew you wished it had never happened.'

Putting his arm round her waist, Warren led her over to a chair, sat in it, and pulled her down on to his lap. 'I wished it hadn't happened *that way*,' he corrected her. 'That day we met,' a reflective smile came into his eyes, 'I went to meet you determined to have the row of the century. But as soon as I saw you I had the wind completely taken out of my sails. You bowled me over.'

Miranda gave him an astonished look. 'You could have fooled me.'

'I intended to. I still thought of you as a predatory headhunter, remember? It wasn't until we went up to York that I realised I wanted to get to know you better, much better.'

Miranda sat up straight, staring at him. 'Are you saying what I think you're saying?'

'Definitely. I knew that you already had a boy-friend, so after getting off to such a bad start I thought that my only hope of getting anywhere with you was to start all over again and take things slowly. But then we got stuck in the snowstorm and things very rapidly got out of hand. When I woke in the morning, I realised that neither of us had been prepared for what happened, for which you'd rightly blame me, and also that you were quite likely to turn on me and accuse me of getting you drunk and taking advantage of you. So you see, when I woke up I thought I'd lost my one chance of happiness—and that was what I was cursing about.'

Miranda's eyes had widened in growing wonder. 'That was why? But I thought—I thought you were angry because you disliked me so much and wished it had never happened.'

'And I thought you were so cold towards me the following morning for the same reason. And I also thought you were in love with your boyfriend and were angry that you'd been unfaithful to him.'

'But then I broke with Graham.'

'Which was the best news I'd had since we met,' Warren said with certainty. 'And when I finally made you admit you were pregnant I knew that I had to grab you before that silly pride of yours made you decide to go it alone. Because I wanted you so much, Miranda. You hadn't been out of my thoughts since the day we met.'

She gazed at him, still not quite able to believe it. 'Why didn't you tell me?'

'Because I was afraid of frightening you off. You were an ambitious career-woman; you seemed to have your life all mapped out. And I wasn't even sure that you wouldn't suddenly change your mind and have an abortion, let alone want a new man in your life.'

Leaning forward, Miranda kissed him lightly. 'There would always be room for your love in my life,' she said simply. Her eyes filled with regret. 'I wish I'd known on our wedding-night; then I wouldn't have been afraid of seeing you turn away from me again.'

Warren smiled at her. 'How about if we have another wedding-night?'

She smiled delightedly. 'Of course. In a couple of weeks. But not at the same place.'

'As a matter of fact I was thinking of having another wedding as well. A real one this time; in a church with all the trimmings. With a cake,' he added with a grin.

Miranda smiled back at him mistily, unafraid now to show the deep love that shone from her eyes. 'I'd like that.' She picked up his hand and kissed it, held it against her cheek. 'But even if we do get married again, I don't think I'll ever be closer to you than I am at this moment. I only wish——' Her voice broke.

'I know.' Warren put his arms round her and gathered her to him as they sat and grieved for the child that they had lost, and thought with hearts full of hope of the children that were yet to come.

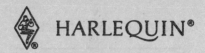

HARLEQUIN®

THE TAGGARTS OF TEXAS!

Harlequin's Ruth Jean Dale brings you
THE TAGGARTS OF TEXAS!

Those Taggart men—strong, sexy and hard to resist...

You've met Jesse James Taggart in FIREWORKS!
Harlequin Romance #3205 (July 1992)

And Trey Smith—he's THE RED-BLOODED YANKEE!
Harlequin Temptation #413 (October 1992)

Now meet Daniel Boone Taggart in SHOWDOWN!
Harlequin Romance #3242 (January 1993)

And finally the Taggarts who started it all—in LEGEND!
Harlequin Historical #168 (April 1993)

Read all the Taggart romances!
Meet all the Taggart men!

Available wherever Harlequin Books are sold.

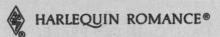

HARLEQUIN ROMANCE®

Some people have the spirit
of Christmas all year round...

People like Blake Connors
and Karin Palmer.

Meet them—and love them!—in
Eva Rutland's
ALWAYS CHRISTMAS.

Harlequin Romance #3240
Available in December wherever
Harlequin books are sold.   HRHX